CURSED IMAGES

Reuben Dendinger

HYPERIDEAN PRESS

Hyperidean Press C.I.C.
www.hyperideanpress.com

Editors: Stewart McCarthy, Richard Porteous
and Udith Dematagoda

Cursed Images / Reuben Dendinger – First Edition September 2023

Cover: *Venus* by Anna Sebastian © 2021

ISBN 978-1-9163767-8-6

Dedicated to Lee Moore

CONTENTS

THE BROOMS OF CARLACK

It was the winter of my senior year in college when I saw the notice for Fannie's first and only public exhibition. *Visions of Carlack—Paintings, Sketches, and Sculpture by Fannie Acheson.* The text, in a whimsical and twisted blackletter, was superimposed on one of Fannie's paintings. I'd never seen the image before, but the style was unmistakable: the dancer's sunken eyes, the faint smile which concealed everything, the sick yellow of the sky.

The location was a gallery in Red Hook. I asked my roommate Misha about it—he was a photographer, and kept up with the art scene—he informed me the gallery was new, and supposedly at the cutting edge. I showed him the notice and he agreed to accompany me to the opening, that very night. Of course, I didn't mention that Fannie was my sister, and that I hadn't seen her in eleven years—it was too much to explain. The fact of our shared last name I shrugged off as a curious coincidence.

Misha and I rented the top floor of a brownstone in Bushwick. With both parents dead, I got my full inheritance as soon as I turned 18. I allowed myself six thousand a month, and typically spent all of it—much of it on the lavish parties I threw in the apartment. It should come as no surprise that I had acquired a lot of friends, the most fashionable I could find, though now I barely remember their faces. The fact is that most of them were completely uninteresting, just like me.

This struck me most acutely during my New Year's Eve party that winter, when at some point in the evening I realized with horror that nobody in attendance was an artist. Filmmakers and digital artists didn't count in my estimation—I wanted painters, and had worked painfully to surround myself with them. All my girlfriends had been painters, and they were my most prized acquaintances, but they had abandoned me first singly and now en masse. They had got sick of me, finally, sensing desperation, or something worse. I panicked at the absurd thought of them all gathered at some other apartment, laughing together about me and my party. As for those loyal friends who had shown up—vapid liberal arts majors and hangers-on—it was only a matter of time before they drifted off as well, and I would be alone.

It became apparent that winter that I was living in a dream, playing out some tired *fin de siècle* cliché lifted from the pages of some novel I skimmed for a seminar. In the gray light of the new year everything felt suddenly drained of significance and reality. I even questioned if my fortune were as substantial as I thought, or if I were living on borrowed money, accumulating a vast debt that one day would come due.

Misha understood everything. At least, he seemed to. We rarely talked about anything real, but we would take drugs together and sit on the roof of the building and look out at the city skyline, and these moments gave me the sense that he understood me somehow and forgave me for everything. I suppose he was my best friend, maybe my only friend. I needed him there with me if I was going to see Fannie.

Fannie's opening was the first Monday in February. It was brutally cold and wet and the sky bulged with lowering gray-white. We were in our favorite café off Myrtle Avenue when I saw the poster. The barista had to call my name three times before I snapped out of my reverie.

After I showed the poster to Misha, we agreed to take a cab to Red Hook after our classes that day and get a drink while we waited for the exhibition to open. Neither of us had spent any time in the area, but Misha consulted the internet and soon had a list of the trendiest bars and restaurants in the neighborhood. We picked one closest to the gallery. I would need more than one drink before seeing Fannie, or those paintings.

I'm not sure exactly how old I was when Fannie first told me about the Brooms of Carlack. After father died I had trouble falling asleep at night, and so our mother told Fannie to keep me company. She was reading to me from some book, in the dim golden halo of my bedside lamp, but neither of us cared much about the story. Fannie paused at a particularly dull moment to yawn, and I took this opportunity to interrupt.

"Fannie," I said. "What *is* a broom?"

As a child I was fascinated by language—the way that abstract sounds, glued together in our mouths and uttered into the world with such ease and carelessness, could represent concepts and things. I went through a period where I stuck on certain words and morphemes, becoming obsessed by them, reciting them like secret mantras, writing them down over and over on pieces of paper in different colors, until through sheer repetition they became detached from their original object and rendered almost meaningless. One such word was *broom*.

The housecleaner who came once a week used a vacuum and a mop to clean the floors, but in a closet in the kitchen there was a broom. It was rarely used, but came out from time to time to sweep the kitchen floor. It was the old-fashioned kind—a bundle of golden straw lashed together, attached to a wooden pole. Old-fashioned, but not old—they sold ones just like it at the hardware store. Still, to me, it was not just a broom, but a *broom*, the thing that witches rode at night, a word which for me was a riddle, a mystery.

I wrote down words that rhymed with it—*gloom, doom, room, tomb*—in circles and radial patterns around the master word in my mantra pages. And in boredom, after school or on the weekend, I would pace around the house chanting "Broom, broom, broom, broom," until my mother would yell and threaten to punish me if I didn't shut up.

"What *is* a broom?"

Fannie had heard my absurd recitations, and seen the pages of scribbled words hanging on the walls of my bedroom (this, of course, was well before mother tore them all down, and forbade me from chanting the magic word ever again). And so Fannie knew precisely what I was asking—not about the mundane object, but about some mystery which its name concealed. She thought it over for a moment, pursing her lips, then closed shut the book in her lap.

"Not broom," she said at last. "*Brooms.*"

"Brooms?"

"That's right." Fannie looked behind her, at my open bedroom door and the light from the hallway. When she turned back round she leaned in, and spoke in a whisper, her consonants smacking and clicking like insects in the hush of her breath. "The Brooms...of *Carlack*. It's a place. Haven't you heard of it?"

I shook my head. I was lying with the blanket pulled up to my chin.

Fannie feigned surprise, cocking her head and letting her jaw drop slightly. She brushed a lock of hair out of her face. "Well, I'll have to tell you all about it. Carlack is where brooms grow wild."

"They grow? Like a plant?"

"That's right. Brooms are shrubs, with yellow flowers in the spring. But most of the year in Carlack they are leafless and dry and brown, dry brambles that will scratch your skin if you walk through them. They cover the ground as far as you can see. And when the wind sweeps across the Brooms they shake and shiver."

"Do people live in Carlack?"

"Oh no. Well, not *normal* people, anyway. Only ghosts and witches live in Carlack. They live in houses made of stone, in fields of poisonous black thistle."

"What do they eat?"

This made Fannie pause. She bit her lip and thought for a moment before going on. "Well," she said, "there are big dandelions…and there are briers that grow, with sweet red roses. People eat those. And there are also black rabbits that live in the briers—people eat those, too."

I asked her to tell me more, but she was running out of steam. The last detail she could think of was the sky, or as she called it, the *skies*.

"The skies?"

"That's right," she said. "They're not like ours. The skies in Carlack are yellow, always yellow…*except for when they turn red.*"

Something about this chilled me. "Red?" I whimpered. "Why do the skies turn red?"

But Fannie couldn't go on. Our mother's voice from the hallway called in to tell us, "Lights out!"

"Next time," Fannie whispered, and with the click of my lamp, all was dark.

By evening the sky had cleared. We arrived in Red Hook in the icy dark with scarves wrapped around our mouths—the frigid air was painful to breathe—at a row of old warehouses overlooking the water. The street was nearly empty and there was very little light from any windows. The eeriness of the scene, the black water gurgling on the spraypainted cement, the warehouses looming with the immense and stupid quiet of their sordid history—it did nothing for my nerves. I was freezing and needed that drink.

Misha led us down an alleyway, to what was allegedly one of the trendiest vodka speakeasies in Brooklyn. The unassuming and unlit entrance was marked only by a faded white cross painted on the door, barely visible in the shadows of the alley.

"They call this place the Tomb," said Misha, his eyes gleaming with delight. "Let's check it out."

The ominous door opened onto a cement stairway which descended into darkness. Had I not been so desperate to get out of the freezing night air, I would have hesitated. But we hurried inside and shut the door behind us, so that then we were immersed in a total darkness that smelled of wet concrete and urine. We turned on the flashlights on our phones.

"Are you sure this is right?" I said as we began our slow descent. "Why is there no light?"

"I told you," said Misha, "it's a speakeasy. It's not supposed to be easy to find. Come on, you know this is sick!"

Thankfully, the smell of urine faded as we descended farther down the staircase, though I occasionally had to avoid stepping on used condoms and broken glass. At last we reached a disused, empty basement. A scan of our flashlights revealed a stack of empty crates laced with cobwebs, and on the opposite wall another door. This, at last, led us to the bar.

After hurriedly removing our coats and winter paraphernalia, we collapsed onto one of the fur-covered sofas. The place was deserted aside from us and the bartender. Misha reviewed the vodka menu on the coffee table while I admired the decorating. It was a cozy, dim place, lit by white exposed bulbs. The walls were covered with various framed prints of macabre art, including one of Francis Bacon's crucifixions, and some work I recognized as that of the Russian occultist painter Denis Forkas. Behind the bar was an impressive array of vodka and aquavit bottles—the place, apparently, served nothing else.

The bartender came around to serve us. He had shoulder-length black hair pushed behind his ears, wire frame spectacles, and was wearing a white Scandinavian-style knitted sweater with a classic black rose pattern trim.

"Welcome," he said in a thick Slavic accent. "My name is Miłosz, I am the owner. Would the gentlemen like to order *wódka.*"

Misha pointed to something on the menu to see if I approved. I didn't know any of the brands, and it was half in foreign alphabets that I couldn't begin to read. The prices were surreal, even by our standards, but I consented with a wave.

"Tell me more about this gallery," I said to Misha, after he'd given our order. "You said before it's one of the most talked about in the city. Why have I never heard of it?"

"Well, it's completely new. Just last year the building was a microbrewery. But I guess the brewers couldn't afford it, with rent going up every year."

"Who owns the gallery?"

Misha shrugged. "Nobody special, I don't think. A daughter of a Wall Street executive, probably. You know how it is. Certainly there's money behind it—all the buzz of the past few months doesn't come cheap."

"So how does an unknown artist land an exhibition at a place like that?"

"The usual way. Money, connections…"

Miłosz returned with our drinks, a shot each of a Finnish and a Latvian vodka, along with a plate of warm black bread and butter.

"Anyway," Misha went on, "I'm excited to see the work. *Visions of Carlack*—what an intriguing title…"

Miłosz dropped the tray a half-inch from the table. It clattered, and one of the shotglasses fell over. He remained frozen there, stooped over the table, staring at the viscous pool of spilled vodka. He trembled faintly, beads of sweat gathering on his forehead. Then, slowly, apparently oblivious to the spillage of his extremely rare and overpriced *wódka*, he stood upright.

Misha and I were stunned. We glanced at each other, and then at Miłosz. A distraught, hazy look had come into his eyes. I thought he must be upset and embarassed by spilling the drink, and I was just about to issue reassurances, to make some kind of joke to help him laugh it off. But then he spoke.

"Carlack," he said, then stopped—the word caught in his throat.

"Yes?" I said, chilled. "The exhibition?"

Miłosz licked his lips. It seemed his mouth had gone suddenly dry. He winced and touched his throat.

"Are you alright?" asked Misha.

"Yes," Miłosz removed his glasses and cleaned them on his sweater. "I'm just…excited. Fannie Acheson. I love her paintings."

By the time we left the Tomb, we'd run up a tab of over six-hundred dollars. That wasn't even counting the *gratis* samples of prized single-estate Polish *wódka* that Miłosz insisted we try, or the handsome tip I left for him. I wasn't even that drunk, and with everything I'd heard I was almost wishing I'd had more.

After our mention of Carlack, Miłosz barely left us alone. He was thrilled we were going to the exhibition, and wanted to tell us all about his relationship with Fannie. Alternately frantic and distracted, he spoke in a confused, elliptical ramble about *wódka*, about painting, about Fannie Acheson, the devil, witchcraft, and his grandmother, who he called *babcia*. It was hard to understand anything he was saying, not only because he occasionally lapsed into Polish, but because he constantly interrupted himself, leaving anecdotes and explanations unfinished, to move abruptly onto another subject. And, anyway, many of his utterances were jumbled and nearly incomprehensible.

The long and short of it was that apparently Fannie had been renting a studio in Red Hook for some time, and she'd been a regular at the Tomb. She never talked much, but sat in the corner with her sketchpad, filling up endless pages with drawings and notes, drinking copiously and sucking on electronic cigarettes. Miłosz, a great admirer of dark and fantastical art, noticed her work, which she always left sitting open on the table when he brought over her drinks (she always drank the cheapest stuff, on the rocks, though even this was hardly cheap). He was so enchanted by her sketches that he offered to buy some. When Fannie mentioned she was a painter, he insisted she show him. In the end he claimed to have bought several of her drawings, and one painting.

When speaking about the paintings, Miłosz seemed to be in pain. He would furrow his brow and rub his eyes, force a laugh, leave the table to get more drinks. While we talked, he drank more vodka then we did, sometimes pouring himself a shot at the bar before he returned to take one with us.

He had nothing to say about the paintings themselves, but only what they reminded him of. Here he would turn to confusing anecdotes about his *babcia* and the bedtime stories she would tell him as a child, and the strange incantations she would whisper in his ear when he got sick. These incantations, which he could only partially translate for us, and which had to do with the wind and the sun and the sky, and with a mythical island and a race of magicians, he seemed to think all this was in some way deeply connected to Fannie's paintings, to Carlack. He repeatedly displayed to us a charm he wore around his neck—an iron key—which he took out from under his sweater and kissed, murmuring something in Polish. He seemed to think we should understand all of this, as if we were all in on some unspoken secret that revolved around Fannie Acheson and Carlack, but he barely noticed how bewildered and unsettled we were by his rambling stories and unbalanced behavior.

"Do you have them here?" I asked him. "The paintings. Are they hanging up?"

This elicited a sharp laugh from Miłosz. To display Fannie's work in public was impossible, he explained. And that was why he wouldn't be visiting the exhibition. He claimed Fannie had asked him to cater the opening, but he had refused. He could look at her paintings one at a time, but to be surrounded by them in a gallery would be impossible. "Totally impossible," he said. "Totally impossible."

I tried to press him about Fannie, but he wouldn't tell me anything more, and at a certain point became suddenly defensive, almost hostile. It was then that I handed him my credit card and we made our exit, up the dark and filthy basement stairs and back into the freezing alleyways of Red Hook.

The last time I saw Fannie was the fight—the big fight, the last fight. The fight that ended with the police arresting Fannie and taking her to a psychiatric hospital. I wasn't told where exactly she was taken and I was not allowed to visit. I was ten.

After everything happened, and Fannie got sent away, I was forced to see a psychiatrist twice a week. I couldn't get any answers from my mother, and so I asked the doctor.

"Why are they doing this? It was just a story."

"Not just a story. There were drawings…"

"So what? It's not real."

"Yes, but sometimes things that aren't real can still be dangerous."

"How?"

"If they scare people, or if they make people do bad things."

The exhibition was over before it started. Apparently, they'd let in a small handful of critics twenty minutes early, so that by the time we got there the event was already being shut down. Cars were pulling out of the parking lot and driving away.

The gallery was right on the water, a short walk from the Tomb. A banner advertised Fannie's exhibition, with a blown-up version of the same design on the flier. As we approached, it was obvious something was wrong, not only from the cars leaving the parking lot, but from the loud confrontation outside the front entrance, which in the frigid darkness was audible from some distance away.

A woman dressed in a flowing black kimono was gesticulating and arguing frantically with a group of people. Voices yelled in tones of denunciation and disgrace. The woman in the kimono covered her face with her hands, sat down in the snow and sobbed.

Misha and I rushed across the snow-covered sidewalk. By the time we reached the gallery, the confusion had only heightened, as newcomers seeking entrance were turned away by a flustered gallery attendant in an overcoat, who was trying to help the distressed woman while keeping the curious visitors from entering the gallery.

"The exhibition is closed for tonight," he cried out meekly to the crowd of visitors while he pulled the sobbing woman to her feet. "Please come back tomorrow."

"Don't come back. Never come back!" howled the inconsolable woman, who I surmised was the gallery owner.

"What's going on?" I asked a couple with matching dyed-black hair and black leather motorcycle jackets. They shrugged, too enthralled by the spectacle to think.

Despite our entreaties, and those of the other prospective attendees, no one was allowed to enter the gallery, and none of our questions were answered. Once the gallery attendant had dragged the hysterical owner inside, the door was locked and the lights were shut out. Muffled screams could be heard from within the brick warehouse as the baffled and disappointed crowd dispersed.

A number of cabs were still idling in the street, their drivers having sensed they'd better hang around. I saw the motorcycle jacket couple climbing back into their cab, and I asked them if we could share it.

"What happened back there?" I repeated after we had piled into the car. The heater was blasting in the cab. It was stifling, and stank of that distinctive taxi cab heater smell, which I found both loathsome and strangely comforting.

"Let's go to a bar," said Misha.

"I've heard there's a vodka speakeasy around here," suggested the woman.

"No," said Misha and I simultaneously.

The couple's names were Oscar and Kitty. We had a drink with them at an old corner grocery converted into one of those garish themed mixology bars, the kind of establishment I despised. It was called The Horror at Red Hook, and served outrageously expensive cocktails named after classic horror films. It was one of those places they'd "been wanting to try." I ordered a bloody mary named after *Angel Heart*, garnished with slices of broiled andouille.

Oscar was a sound engineer and Kitty was a chocolatier. Toward the end of our drink, I asked them how they'd heard about the exhibition. Kitty claimed to be part of a "coven," a secret association of witches. This, in itself, was nothing too unusual. But she told us that it was from her "sisters" that she'd heard about Fannie Acheson and Carlack.

"Is Fannie a witch?" I asked.

"I don't think so," said Kitty with a curious twist of her mouth, as she pensively fingered the swizzle stick of her *Suspiria*-themed blood-orange negroni. "I think she's…something else."

"What do you mean?"

But she would say nothing more, nor would she provide any details about her supposed coven or her practice of witchcraft. The conversation turned back to other things, and soon we had finished our drinks and I was anxious to leave. I paid everyone's tab while Misha ordered a taxi on his phone.

On our way back to the apartment, Misha and I both did as much internet research as our addled brains permitted. Fannie, the gallery and its owner, New York City witchcraft, Polish folklore, Carlack. We turned up almost nothing about Fannie except for what I already knew—she had briefly attended a prestigious art college before being expelled in her third year. As for the gallery, it was indeed owned by a young heiress—the daughter of real estate money. Her name was Lily Price, and her father Zachary apparently owned the warehouse and a large chunk of Red Hook along with sizable tracts of the most aggressively "up and coming" Brooklyn neighborhoods. His name mostly appeared in connection with lawsuits against allegedly racist rent-gouging and heavy-handed evictions, and it seemed his office was a frequent target for protests by anti-gentrification activists. Lily herself was a non-entity—she'd graduated with a degree in art history from NYU, put in her time as a writer at a couple of elite magazines, then opened the gallery only about four months ago.

As for the rest—witchcraft, covens, otherworldly rumors, everything hinted at by Miłosz and Kitty—the internet was a rabbit-hole of bad information we were too exhausted to parse. But when we made it home, I poured us both a glass of wine and told Misha the truth—that Fannie was my sister.

I was too tired and nervous to go into any detail, but I at least told him the basic facts. Fannie had been incarcerated in a mental institution as a teenager, and my mother had prohibited me from visiting her or contacting her in any way. After my mother died and I turned eighteen, I made a brief attempt to track her down, but came up with nothing. At that point she'd already been kicked out of school and had apparently disappeared without a trace— until now.

At first Misha was horrified, but soon he seemed to regard the entire thing as a tragic and unholy prank of which I was the victim, and he gave me the awkward condolences that seemed appropriate. After this, I went to bed, but hardly slept all night.

"Has art lost the ability to shock? In this late era, it seems, every trick has thankfully been exhausted. Today's audiences are hardly capable of being scandalized. For better or worse, bourgeois morality has been debunked. We're all heathens now, or so I thought. But apparently, beneath the surface of our apocalyptic libertinism, there still exists some shred of good taste, some instinct to defend what remains of civilization and sanity. How else to explain the reaction of myself and the others who briefly witnessed Fannie Acheson's debut?"

This was how the review began. Despite the attendance of several critics, it was the only write-up of Fannie's opening night that had been published. It was written by a reputable critic in a middling magazine, but the review was unhinged, almost hysterical in its denunciation of Fannie's art, which was described variously as "obscene," "ghoulish," and "diseased." The proportions were "nauseating," the use of color "depraved," and the brushstrokes "sadistic...evincing an attitude of sardonic contempt for the entire world."

"The work contains no sex or violence, no religious or political blasphemy," the reviewer wrote. "But there is, throughout all of Acheson's work, a blasphemy of a different order—a sick barbarism, a spiritual lewdness, at which words can scarcely hint. In the haunted eyes and obscene smiles of her ghosts, in the lurid skies and diabolical flora of Carlack's bleak and cursed vistas, the viewer is overwhelmed with the suggestion of a vast, sweeping and yet unspoken, indeed unspeakable, metaphor concealing a grand cabalistic and nightmarish horror beyond imagination."

All of the prose was like this—it was disturbing, almost unreadable. Concluding the short review, the critic declared "Fannie Acheson's career began and ended in a single night, an evening which, like an unwholesome dream, will, I pray, soon be mercifully forgotten by everyone involved."

I showed the review to Misha, who was convinced it was some kind of sick joke. When I called the magazine, I was told the critic had been fired shortly after the review's publication, and the editors were preparing an apology for their next issue. Apparently the reviewer was a recovering alcoholic, and in the last few days had dramatically relapsed. After his dismissal he reportedly retreated to a long-term rehab clinic in Rhode Island.

The exhibition, *Visions of Carlack*, was canceled and the gallery shut down. As the legend of the cursed paintings exploded, inflamed by the deranged review, by rumors spread by the other attendees, and by the closure of the gallery, Lily Price went into hiding.

Somehow, people got the idea that she was involved in some kind of secret cult. Human trafficking, black market organ transplants, elite finance, ancient myth, extraterrestrial contact—the internet's collective paranoia found in the Fannie Acheson scandal a thrilling new chapter for its mosaic fantasia. Lily Price, her social media accounts dogged by death threats and conspiratorial rants, deleted her online presence and relocated to Saint Martin, or possibly Martinique, to wait until the affair blew over.

It was funny, I thought, that her father, a criminal by any account, enriching himself by plundering the city and throwing poor people out of their homes, could apparently eat dinner wherever he liked without fearing for his life. His enemies, whatever they thought of him, had some measure of decency. But there are some people whose unlaundered garments demand to be washed in human blood. And in the end it doesn't really matter whose blood it is.

Images surfaced on the internet of paintings and sculptures, draped in beige sheets, being moved out of the gallery in the middle of the night by armed security personnel into unmarked vans.

The storm of bile and hateful accusations which descended on Lily Price reminded me, of course, of my mother, our mother, and the things she would say to Fannie when we were children. Among the vile things mother said and did, she often called Fannie a witch. "What are you whispering about now, you little witch?"

When father was killed in a car accident, mother started taking diazepam and drinking heavily. She did nothing all day but drink wine, watch television, and sleep. Occasionally she'd find men on the internet to take her out, and she'd return the next morning wearing her clothes from the night before. Before going on a date, she'd sometimes take me aside to reassure me.

"Don't worry," she would say. "I'm not gonna marry him. Nobody is getting Daddy's money. It's all for you, sweetheart."

Even before things got bad, it was apparently out of the question that Fannie would inherit anything. It was like, from my mother's perspective, she only existed as a shadow. Ever since I was small, I knew mother didn't like Fannie, but I never understood why.

Fannie wasn't a shadow to me. She practically raised me, until she got sent away—after that, I was on my own. When mother was drunk, which was all the time, Fannie did the cooking or ordered takeout. When I had questions about the world, or needed help, I asked Fannie. And at night she put me to sleep, whispering her strange stories to me as she drew pictures in her sketchbook. Pictures of Carlack.

I knew it wasn't real, that it was all a game. But I became obsessed. Obsessed with the brooms, the sound of them, the sensation of bristles rushing in the wind. Obsessed with the scythes of the witches in black harvesting the brambles to fashion into magic broomsticks. Obsessed with the ghoulish courtiers of the castle of Count Carlack, their deranged jests, their alien rituals. Obsessed with the Sweeper, the great ghost who lived in the wind—or perhaps he was the wind? I was never quite entirely sure, and Fannie never really explained, only hinted at who and what he was. A king? Magician? Vampire? The devil himself? All I knew about the Sweeper was that the witches would go to whisper and sacrifice to him at the Sabbath on the haunted moor. And one day, Fannie told me, he would come, the Sweeper, when the skies turned red, and at last he would sweep everything away.

In the days and weeks after the canceled exhibition, I was in a bad way. But Misha insisted I go ahead with my planned calendar of parties.

"It'll cheer you up!" he said. "I'm inviting those girls from Parsons. They're bringing a *lot* of ketamine."

I allowed him to persuade me. I hated winter in New York even in the best of times, and despite an intense instinct to hide myself away with my dread and my memories, I was desperate to be surrounded by people who liked me. "Those girls from Parsons" were artists, and eminenly fashionable—perhaps their presence would help me reclaim some of my lost standing from the New Year's Eve catastrophe.

As always, we provided tiered arrival times to guests from different social groups, ensuring that the party was populated with stylish and attractive personalities from the beginning so as to firmly establish the correct aura. New people, especially, had to be suitably impressed by the mix of genders and subcultures on display, all mingling in an atmosphere of discreet, tasteful hedonism.

It was this last quality that I almost spoiled by failing to pace myself at the beginning. I was eager to forget about Fannie and Carlack, to get everything associated with it out of my mind completely, so when some of Misha's friends arrived with an antique hookah and a plastic bag of mushrooms, I poured us all some craft beer ($28 per twelve-ounce bottle) and we set to work. By the time the girls from Parsons arrived the apartment was comfortably full with warm and laughing bodies and the party was electric, or at least I thought it was—I was so high it's hard to be sure.

Misha introduced me to the Parsons sisters when they arrived, but now I only remember one of them. She was gifted with one of those stunning and dubious names that eccentric liberals once gave their children—I believe it may have been Swanlake. Her style was almost unbearably immaculate—a mullet, Carhartt jacket, Doc Martens, a silver septum piercing, hand tattoos. Underneath the jacket, which she notably kept wearing indoors until it became uncomfortably warm, she was wearing a crimson floral dress over a black turtleneck sweater. I probably made an idiot of myself, stoned and tongue-tied, but I don't think she cared.

Somehow I found myself on a sofa with Swanlake. She was telling me all about her art, which had something to do with the internet. She was talking about the end of art and the end of the world. It was probably all completely trite, but in my present condition I perceived in every word and phrase a sublime profundity. Her discourse drove at the essence of things—everything was "essentially" something. "We're all essentially alienated from ourselves," she said. "Our culture is essentially still a Christian one."

I nodded knowingly while she went on like this, grasping for some way to intervene and demonstrate my intelligence. Finally, she said something like, "At this point, we've crossed too many boundaries. Ecologically, economically, spiritually. We're doomed, essentially."

"Yes," I said at last, licking my dry lips. "I'm afraid you're right."

Swanlake blinked, surprised and flattered. "Really?"

I cleared my throat, not entirely confident of everything I had just signed off on. But I wanted her badly. "Yes. Absolutely."

She bit her lower lip. "Want to do some ketamine?"

We went into my bedroom and I kissed her neck and the shaved sides of her skull while she cut lines on my dresser.

I showed her my antique German ivory cocaine snorter, which normally delights everyone. But Swanlake took it into her hands and examined it and with a devastating sweep of her eyelashes looked from me, to the snorter, and back to me, and seemed to pass judgment against the artifact and against me and my entire existence. The last thing I remember, before I exited the room and my body and my identity completely, is insufflating ketamine while she pulled her dress over her head.

The big fight, the last fight, the night which got Fannie arrested and sent away, began with me, with my dream. I barely remember the dream itself now, but everything that happened afterward is clear as day.

"The Sweeper! The Sweeper! He's sweeping me up! *MOMMY! HE'S SWEEPING ME UP! HE'S SWEEPING ME UP! MOMMY?*"

Mother rushed into the bedroom and turned on the lights. I was inconsolable, sitting upright in bed, screaming at the top of my lungs. Mother, frantically and fruitlessly trying to calm me, started crying as she clutched me to her chest. I kept screaming for a long time, repeating again and again that the sky had turned red and the Sweeper was coming to sweep us all away.

When it became clear that my nightmare was the product of Fannie's stories, which she'd been whispering to me for over a year, mother became hysterical. She raided Fannie's bedroom, emptied out every drawer from the dresser, ripped down dresses from the closet. She was searching for hidden sketchbooks and diaries and she found them. I was there, watching with dread as Fannie howled and cried while mother tore apart her room. One book was filled with drawings of a boy from school— lots and lots of drawings. Mother, still weeping, laughed cruelly while she leafed through it before flinging it over her shoulder like a piece of garbage. And then she found the other sketchbook, the drawings of Carlack.

I had seen some of them before: the ghosts, the ballerinas, the magicians, the floating dream-like rituals amid the brooms. And there were ones I hadn't seen: naked witches flying on broomsticks, people flinging themselves over the sides of cliffs. Some of them Fannie had colored with markers, with the distinctively sickening palette of streaked umber, jaundice, and black, speckled with blood.

Mother paged through the images with horror, and then with delirious and decisive purpose stormed from the room, roughly pushing me aside. We followed her to the bathroom, where she cast the artwork into the tub and then retrieved a jug of bleach from the cabinet under the sink. Fannie grabbed mother's arm and tried to stop her, and mother struck her in the face, and then again repeatedly on the back while Fannie cowered.

"You're going to burn in hell, you little witch," she said as she emptied the jug of bleach onto the sketchpad. Ink hemorrhaged from the paper in the froth of poison. When she was done, she hurled the plastic jug at Fannie, so that the remnants of bleach splashed across her face and arm. Afraid of what mother would do next, I followed her into the other room while Fannie desperately tried to wash the chemical off her skin.

In the living room, mother was phoning the police. "Yes, my daughter is mentally disturbed. She's threatening me and my son."

We lived in a neighborhood where the police came quickly. There was nowhere for Fannie to run, and she knew that.

"I never want to see you again," said mother.

"Oh, don't worry," replied Fannie. "You won't."

Four men arrived, with shackles and tasers at hand—that's what it took, apparently, to subdue a teenage girl. But Fannie didn't resist. She gave herself up. But amid all the screaming and the crying, she got in the final words, the last words I heard her speak:

"The Sweeper *will* come. And he will sweep *everything away!*"

I came to around three in the morning. The apartment was empty. I was sitting on the sofa, cradling a bottle of blue sports drink. Misha walked past me, carrying empty beer bottles back to the kitchen. I flagged him down.

"Are you feeling okay?"

"What happened?"

"You scared us," he said. It was clear he was embarrassed, exhausted, but truly shaken. "You were ranting. About brooms. About fire. The witch's sabbath. And your sister…some people had seen the fliers. It touched a nerve."

I wet my parched throat with another deep sip of sugar water. "What are you saying?" I repeated. "What happened?"

Misha shook his head.

After my humiliation at the party, I became committed to locating Fannie. I hired a private investigator, the best available. I myself contacted Kitty from the night of the exhibition, and she agreed to meet me for a drink.

When I told her that Fannie was my sister she was sympathetic and much more open. She confessed to me that ever since the disastrous opening night she'd been plagued, like so many others, by nightmares of the Carlack flier. The anxiety was so bad she'd begun seeing a therapist.

I listened attentively, and when the moment was right I insisted she tell me everything she knew about witchcraft and about Fannie. It was as if, somehow, my search for my sister would somehow bring peace to Kitty's nightmares—we both felt this without stating it. Nonetheless, she held back—until I offered to pay for her therapy visits.

Between what Kitty told me and what the private investigator was able to gather, I was eventually able to track down Fannie. For the past several years she had been living under a series of assumed names in different parts of the city. She left Red Hook after the exhibition and now was holed up in a studio in Brownsville. One of her only points of contact was with the networks of modern witchcraft practitioners from whom she purchased certain rare and semi-illicit botanical preparations. Apparently, Fannie's sketches had become something like religious artifacts, coveted by magicians and circulated within the ranks of New York's secret witch-cults for use in black magic rituals and initiations.

I had no idea how Fannie might respond to my showing up on her doorstep. But I knew that if I tried to contact her in advance—a phone call, a letter, an intermediary—she might disappear again, maybe even leave the city, or the country. However shocking it might be for her, I felt I had no choice.

It was in the evening after a day of classes. I had the taxi drop me off two blocks away, then I circled around and ducked into an alleyway to hide and wait. I told myself it was in case I had been followed, though I knew in reality I was simply afraid.

Her number was the top floor of the building. I rang the electric doorbell and waited.

The sound of strange music and the smell of incense emanated from her door. I waited, then buzzed the doorbell again, and knocked. Finally, the door opened a crack, the chain lock still fastened, and an eye peered out.

"What do you want?"

"Fannie," I said. "It's me."

She looked at me for a moment, and I suppose recognized me, but my identity seemed to make no impression. "And?" she repeated. "What do you want?"

"I just want to talk. Let me in, please. I'm freezing."

She shut the door, unlocked it, opened it again and let me inside. The studio was completely empty except for an easel, a pile of canvases and painting supplies, some scattered books, a refrigerator, a small stereo, and an old mattress on the floor. Aside from a lamp trained on the easel, there was no light. Fannie finished locking and bolting the door, and then walked past me to the fridge.

"Do you want a drink?"

She poured us both some white wine into coffee mugs. And then she leaned against the refrigerator and stared at me while she drank. She was wearing white overalls, smattered with paint, her dark hair pulled back in a ponytail. She looked much the same—dark circles under blank, distracted eyes; velvet lips in a tight, unforgiving smile. She cupped the mug of wine with both hands as if she were warming herself with hot tea.

"What do you want to talk about?" she said with subtle mocking levity.

"Your paintings made quite the stir," I said idiotically.

Fannie laughed. "Yeah, the world wasn't ready for Carlack, was it? Or, I should say, *their* world," she added. "*Their* world wasn't ready."

My eyes were drawn to the painting on the easel. A crimson field, streaked with blacks and browns, and looming over everything…

"The Sweeper…"

"Yes," she said, showing her teeth. "What do you think? It's for my next show."

"You can't possibly—" I started.

"Of course I can. It will be a private exhibition. I'm in high demand, in certain circles." She smiled unpleasantly. "Why are you here?"

"I want to give you your share of the inheritance. The full half. I placed it in a trust fund on your behalf, it's been accumulating interest—"

"I don't want Dad's fucking money," Fannie snarled, her lips curled with disdain. "I get by just fine on my own. Can't you tell?"

My lip trembled. I felt like crying for the first time in many years. "I want you to have it," I said. "Please, I can—"

"I know the real reason you came here," she said with an accusing smile, her eyes livid. "You want to know why the skies turn red."

Speechless, bewildered, stung—I looked away, spun toward the cold and shadowy corners of the bare hideout.

"You'll understand," she said, with a brutal, demented calm. "Soon everyone will understand."

"Please," I begged, wiping my eyes with the sleeve of my sweater. "Please let me give you the money."

"I don't want your filthy money. Everything I have is mine. I earned it."

"Fine then," I said. "Have it your way."

Years passed. Brooklyn got worse. Everything got worse, slowly at first, and then faster and faster. I still live in the same brownstone in Bushwick. I bought the building soon before the real estate market collapsed (not the small crash you're thinking of, I mean when it truly collapsed, for the last time). What remains of the money is barely enough to pay the expenses. Too many bad investments. But whatever anyone offers me—and they do, the offers pour in daily, in the mail, online, by phone—I refuse to sell any of Fannie's work. Yes, the art market imploded along with everything else, but Fannie's paintings were impervious—they only become more valuable with every year. I paid between fifty and a hundred-thousand dollars per painting, more for the sculptures, and around a thousand each for a large portfolio of charcoal and pencil sketches. Do you think it was a good price?

No more parties, of course—now I drink alone. I've been alone since the night I brought home the artwork and told Misha he had to leave. It would be completely irresponsible to expose anyone to these paintings. It seems I'm the only one who can stand to be surrounded by them. And I refuse to put them away. The main room is devoid of furniture. The walls are covered in Fannie's work. It's a private gallery which nobody is permitted to see. Many try to, of course—they find out, one way or another, and they beg me, offer money and strange gifts, just to spend an hour amid the *Visions of Carlack*. But it's impossible. Totally impossible.

The doctors say it's killing me, the vodka. That my liver will turn black and my skin turn yellow. But I don't mind watching myself die. It's like this city, and this planet. I never had any love for any of it, not really.

The first exhibition served its purpose. It implanted the nightmare of Carlack in the world, and drew to Fannie the audience she wanted. Of course she went on painting and drawing, still she goes on today. Not just Carlack anymore—her work now has no boundaries, no borders.

We're all living in Fannie's time now. I don't look out the window anymore, but I think we're living in Fannie's world.

I can't say I'm anything other than afraid, lonely, miserable. I try not to think about the past or the future anymore. But at least Fannie is free. I know she is out there free and flying in the blood-red sky.

THE NECROMANCER'S DRIVER

The first skull was traded to me by a former acquaintance in exchange for cocaine. The older I got, the less interested I was in drugs. But a human skull? It's not that I wanted it, not really—I just wanted to look at it, to hold it. The acquaintance in question was a musician, a drummer. I don't know where he got the skull, or why; if it was used on stage with his heavy metal band, in private Satanic rites, or if it was just a morbid decoration he kept around to impress visitors. Whatever the case, he had outgrown it, so to speak. And so it fell into my hands.

Nothing compares to holding an authentic human skull. To know that it once housed a man's brain—his perceptions, memories, personality, desires, hallucinations—and was attached by a neck to an entire mobile, living body. It is immensely moving, a silent scream of life and death, the immediacy and ultimate absurdity of existence. And it never gets old.

The skull lived in an old plastic storage bin underneath the floorboards in my bedroom. For the most part, it stayed hidden, except when I took it out to hold and ponder while I drank my cheap Canadian whiskey.

About six months went by like that. And then the drummer—the one who traded me the skull in the first place—got an inquiry, which he passed along to me. Someone wanted to buy the skull for $1000. So I made the deal, and the guy—another musician type, a guitarist— paid me in a stack of twenties. I bought myself a case of nice beer and thought about the skull while I drank.

That night a quick internet search confirmed my suspicions. There was a demand for skulls, and it was a seller's market.

Money was short in those days. After high school, I worked at the cannery until it shut down. Then it was odd jobs, restaurants, a bit of this and that. Sometimes on the margin of legal, but nothing heavy. I considered myself lucky to wind up living where I could keep a low profile and not worry about a pain-in-the-ass landlord. A handful of punks and eccentrics lived in trailers and cottages on a stretch of land outside of town. It wasn't a commune, just a living situation—convenient for the time.

In a cottage across the way, on the hill on the other side of the garden where some people were growing vegetables and pot, that's where Imogen lived. She made money by selling hand-woven crafts on the internet. She would sit and weave in the sun on the top of the hill with her dog. Sometimes she would stand there in the light looking off toward the highway or toward the forest, and I would watch her from down by the blackberries where I sometimes sat in a plastic chair to drink beer, and I would think to myself that she looked like a sorceress or a queen from the ancient past.

I was surviving, but without a steady income I was completely broke and I needed to pay off some debts and put some money into my car. And so that's how I got into graverobbing. At the time it seemed like easy money. The dead don't need their bones anymore, do they?

There are certain small cemeteries in the country where the job is easy. I stuck with the oldest graves, because I figured the flesh and everything would be completely rotted away—I wanted clean bones. I picked graves at the edges of the lot, underneath trees where the grass doesn't grow and it's harder to notice when the soil's been upset.

Sometimes I found valuables, like rings and pocket watches, but for some reason I felt guilty about snatching these. That would be stealing. I can't say for certain why the skull felt different. I'd read somewhere, maybe in Tacitus, that the ancient Germans would keep the skulls of enemies slain in battle arrayed as prizes in their homes. It's grisly, yeah, but there's something noble about it, a kind of respect.

I sold the skulls online, cleaned, wrapped in plastic bubbles, boxed, and labeled "Fragile— antique." I contacted the guitarist to whom I'd sold my first skull, and told him if he knew anyone else in the market, I was the man. After a handful of online sales, I received word from him. He knew someone who knew someone, he said, that needed something. Not a skull, but something else. A hand of glory. The left hand of a murderer, convicted and hanged, cut off and preserved, then fitted with a candle made from the fat of the deceased—that was the hand of glory. As you might imagine, this gruesome object was traditionally ascribed with great magic powers. I was amazed that anyone could want such a thing, and equally sure that it would be impossible to obtain.

My violations of the country graves had so far gone unnoticed. The money was real, and I didn't mind the work. And so despite my skepticism, I told the guitarist he could pass along my number.

The sorcerer insisted I meet him at his house. It was clear he needed to impress me, as he made us drink expensive brandy in his study, on leather chairs, surrounded by leather-bound books. The sorcerer himself was middle-aged, his hair prematurely white. He was a retired musician who now wrote books on black magic and witchcraft, and he was well-connected in those circles. I sat and drank his drinks while he presented me with his collection of human skulls carved with magic sigils. He was eager to know what I thought of them, and I tried to give an impression of expertise.

And then we spoke of hands of glory, and I confessed my ignorance of how to acquire such an item. For one thing, murderers were no longer hanged, and if they had been long ago their hands would surely be nothing but bone, whereas the magic required pickled flesh. But the sorcerer explained that for his purposes these specifications were more flexible. Execution by hanging wasn't necessary—a suicide would suffice. And in those days there were plenty.

What about the murder? Wasn't the hand supposed to be that of a killer? But the sorcerer explained that suicide is indeed the taking of a human life, the crime which is its own punishment. As for the candle, it needn't be made *entirely* from human fat, just so long as there was some mixed in. And so all that was needed, really, was the left arm of a suicide, recently committed, from which both hand and fat could be taken.

I wasn't keen on dealing with corpses. Skeletons were one thing, but the thought of sawing flesh made me nauseous. We negotiated my price, and I made the old man agree to pay for a lawyer if I got caught by the police. I used the newspapers to track the latest suicides and waited until one struck a remote community. It didn't take long. I wore a disposable respirator to deal with the smell and brought along a saw. These I dumped in a river and burned my clothes when the night was done. I didn't like the idea of that fresh DNA on any of my possessions. The body was a man's, roughly the same age as the sorcerer, probably laid off from the lumber mill when it closed last year. I timed the operation for the night of a snow, so when I covered everything up and left there with the arm wrapped in painter's tarp, a nice couple inches were still to fall and by the morning everything would have been clean and white.

The sorcerer looked at me with great reverence when I brought him the arm. He paid me my fee, and then offered to put me in touch with a friend of his, a private publisher of custom books.

It's strange how fast it all happened—in just a span of two months, I'd gone from collecting old skulls to harvesting human skin for the binding of magical books. But someone has to do these things, and the money was too good to pass up. Once I had fixed up my car, paid back some debts, and bought some nice things for the house, I opened a savings account, and began to buy gold coins that I hid underneath the floorboards where I used to keep my skull. I bought an AR-15 and lots of ammunition. You could never be too sure in those days. I had to look out for myself, and I often dreamed idly about buying some land of my own one day and settling down with Imogen and a couple of dogs.

The publisher owned a small, secret bookstore in the city, tucked in a dark alley behind an unmarked door. I liked to sit there and look through his collection of strange volumes. Black magic barely interested me, except the parts that involved the use of dead bodies, to which I took a craftsman's interest. I was much keener on the stories, bound in cloth and leather, some embossed with silver or gold; ancient stories, modern stories, about strange gods and distant planets, dreams of unique and striking symbols, mixed with arcane philosophical theories, streaks of horror, science fiction, and sex.

I went farther and farther afield for the publisher, sometimes taking up odd requests from the sorcerer as well. I didn't want to attract any heat, of course, so I had to stop digging around close to home. I used different cars, wore disguises, drove far out two days in advance and circled back round to the spot. Perhaps I took it all too seriously, but still today I'm proud of the fact I was never caught.

One day a strange man came into the shop, a customer. The publisher, busy at work in the basement, had warned me there'd be an appointment, and asked I take care of it.

The man was tall, and like many in those circles (including, now, myself) dressed completely in black. He wore a mask, porcelain and completely solid black aside from the frightening crimson circles painted on the eyes; there were no eyeholes and it was not clear if or how he saw anything. He was wearing a black turtleneck sweater, blazer, and gloves. I had seen eccentric customers come and go in the book shop, but even in a place like this, I thought his appearance excessive. The ensemble might have been ridiculous, were not the impression he gave so chilling. His age was impossible to determine, and he spoke with a deep, cold timbre that was like the groaning of dark pipes.

He had reserved for purchase a book on necromancy, freshly made by the man downstairs.

"I take it you are the one who supplied the skin for this binding," he said, when I had taken the volume from its place and displayed it for him.

His words chilled me. Goosepimples ran up my arms and neck. If he were a cop it would have been all over right then and there.

I said nothing. He ran his gloved hand along the surface of the book. "I need someone like you," he said. "Come work for me."

Doing what, I asked him cautiously. I noticed the publisher in the basement doorway, peering out, watching us, nervously wiping his hands on a towel. It was obvious then he had known this was coming, and I felt faintly betrayed by his cowardice in leaving me alone with this ghoul.

Doing what, I asked again.

"Driving."

As it turned out, it really was as simple as that. All I had to do was drive. The necromancer never asked that I help with his procedures, or even help with lifting the bodies or cleaning the car—my colleague, the processor, took care of all that. I was never invited into the laboratory, nor did I want to be. All I did was drive.

For whatever reason, the necromancer's procedures had to be carried out in a moving vehicle. I never understood why, and I never asked. Cars were never mentioned in the necromantic books I perused at the shop, but then again, I didn't read them closely, and I didn't have the education or the patience for allegory. Of course, nearly anyone can drive a car. But he wanted someone who was comfortable in this world. Someone he could trust, someone who wouldn't get nauseous around dead bodies.

I don't know where the bodies came from. I had nothing to do with procuring them. Some, I think, were obtained purely for the sake of experimentation. But others were brought by clients, who paid the necromancer for his services. That's how he was able to pay me and the processor so well. I never knew who the processor was. Like the necromancer, I never saw his face. He wore a mask exactly like the necromancer's except with painted eyes that were white instead of crimson. Whenever we worked, he wore a black butcher's smock and vinyl gloves. I sometimes wondered what his story was, how he ended up in this line of work—if it was by accident, like me, or if he was chasing some dark science or passion of his own. I never knew, because in all the time I worked with him I never heard him utter a single word.

We only worked at night. The necromancer's laboratory was in the old industrial park on the outskirts of town. Near the derelict cannery where I used to work there were some disused buildings, abandoned for many years. I would go at the appointed time, park my car and start up the necromancer's car, an antique four-door Chrysler. The front passenger seat was rear facing, and the back seats were always covered with fresh tarp. I wore gloves and a respirator, though for whatever reason I was never offered one of the demonic masks that my co-worker and our employer invariably wore.

I would start the car, get it warm. And then the necromancer would appear at the door. Sometimes, a client would be with him—sometimes frightened, sometimes grim and business-like—though often he was alone, in his dark clothes and mask, carrying his antique leather physician's valise. And he would then be followed by the processor, masked and wearing his rubber smock and gloves, and carrying over his shoulder a dead body wrapped in black plastic and duct tape.

Why did we have to drive? It wasn't the night air, because the windows were always kept tightly shut. And it had nothing to do with direction or speed. I drove out into the country, either into the woods or out into farmland. Sometimes I'd pick a stretch of road and follow it all night until it was time to turn around. Sometimes I'd cut a wide loop, or crisscross backroads and shortcuts. I got a map and familiarized myself with every road in the area. Sometimes I'd plan a route, sometimes I'd improvise. None of it seemed to matter—as long as I didn't stop.

As I drove out away from the laboratory, the processor started his work. The necromancer sat in the front passenger seat, which as I said was backwards so he could direct the proceedings, and the processor worked in the back with the body. As far as I know, the necromancer never touched the bodies. I never saw him lay a finger on a single one of our "subjects," as he called them. But he directed the processor's every move with his voice.

I barely understood a word of what the necromancer said during this process. He used so much Latin, I suppose both from medical and occult terminology, that it was impossible for me to follow what he was saying. I was curious, but satisfied to remain ignorant. I wasn't apprenticing at this stuff. I was there to get paid and go home, and I regarded the whole job, at the time, as highly temporary. What I know of the process, I know from stealing glances in the rearview mirror.

The processor would open the necromancer's valise, which contained a variety of knives, surgical tools, and glass bottles. And then, at the necromancer's direction, he began his work, first by unwrapping the naked body from the plastic, and then by cutting it open from the navel to the chest. The first subject was a woman. It was only after driving several times for the necromancer that I realized that each one of his subjects was female.

The process proceeded with the removal of various internal organs, all described with voluminous Latin by the necromancer. Whether this was instruction, narration, or a magical incantation, I have no idea—I suspect it was some combination of all three.

The processor placed the organs in a plastic tray. When he had done this, he then set to work on them with various tools. I'm uncertain, but I believe he may have been inscribing them with words or signs. After this, the organs were replaced in the body, and the abdomen was carefully sewn up tight.

The end of the process was perhaps the strangest of all. The processor took a bottle of spirits from the valise—80 proof alcohol, distilled by the necromancer himself in the laboratory—and poured it into the subject's mouth. And then the necromancer would utter the words: "And now she has become real." And that was it.

When we returned to the lab, the processor carried the body back into the laboratory. I didn't know what happened after that. The necromancer paid me in cash. Afterward, I changed my clothes and later burned them. The spirits used in the process were bottled in green glass stamped with attractive Old-World labels. The necromancer sometimes offered me cases of the stuff for free and I took it. At home I drank heavily and tried to forget the night's work with games, films, music, pornography. I liked guitar music, slow and low, droning, rumbling, hypnotic. I waited and listened for freedom in the sudden pinch or twist of distortion.

I never planned on keeping it up for long. After a while I started to feel restless, ready to leave the necro game entirely. Graves, bodies, black magic—I'd had my fill. I couldn't let it become my life. There was a time, not so long in the past, when I went to parties, live music, galleries, clubs. I had friends, women. There were late nights, jokes, memories.

In my room alone, I drank and dreamed of better days.

Weeks and months went by. I drove for the necromancer and I still leafed through old books in the shop, but the publisher understood I didn't want to bother digging for him anymore, and his trade would have to lapse into ordinary vellum. But one night, when I wasn't working, I drove out to an old country cemetery and dug. Of course, driving paid far better than when I was hunting bodies. The dirt, the sweat, the risk, none of it seemed worthwhile now compared to driving for the necromancer. But I suppose part of me missed the thrill of it. And more than that, I wanted a skull.

It was late in the winter, almost spring. Imogen never did her weaving outside anymore in the cold and so I had to imagine her, inside where it was warm. I don't know for certain how the fire started. It must have been an old blanket or a piece of clothing thrown over the wood stove. Maybe she got wet outside in the cold and put something there to dry, and forgot about it, and something caught fire.

I had been drinking that night, like I did almost every night. I was listening to music and drinking and staring at my skull. I kept it in the same box where the first skull used to live, now on a bed of American and Canadian dollars and Mexican pesos. I was gazing into those black cavities of its former eyes and dreaming about the future and the past and about the beautiful unreal stories from the magic books, dreaming about Imogen. And then I heard the barking of Imogen's dog.

From my window I could see her cottage. I pulled back the curtain and saw nothing but a hand of orange flame glowing on the hill.

I screamed to wake up the others who lived on the property, and seized the fire extinguisher from the closet and raced outside and up to the burning image. Imogen's dog was waiting for me outside and ran with me to the fire, barking frantically. It quickly became obvious that the flames were too much to combat. And so I burst through the flaming door.

What had happened to Imogen? Intoxication, suicide, or a sleep so near to death that its flaming triumph was barely noticed. She lay on her bed, her body engulfed in fire.

With a blast of the extinguisher, I sprayed her with chemical foam. And then I clutched her in my arms and pulled her over my shoulder and was out into the blur of smoke and snow. The others were there, shouting, calling the fire department. I collapsed Imogen into the snowy grass and wiped the foam from her face. There was no doubt that she was dead. Her face ravaged and blackened by the fire, she had no pulse and no breath. I gave her mine, tried to force air into her lungs, to pump her blood with chest compressions, but it was useless.

I knew I had to be quick, because an ambulance could arrive at any moment. I left the others to deal with the fire. I took Imogen to my car, and I went into my room and took out all my boxes of gold and money. The dog chased after me, still barking, chasing the car even as I sped away down the highway towards town. I dialed the necromancer's number until he answered. Imogen's body, still smoking, filled my car with the smell of charred flesh, hair, and fabric.

Outside the laboratory, I showed him the body. He waved a hand over her disfigured face, her melted skin, her ruined hair. I opened the bins of treasure and threw them at his feet, spilling cash and clattering coins, and the skull there with it.

Take everything, I told him. Take it all. Just bring her back to life.

To life—is that what the process did? The truth was, I'd never seen a subject afterward. I had no idea what happened to them, not really. But whatever chance I was taking, or wasting, I could see no other choice.

The processor appeared with us outside, and he took Imogen's body to prepare her while the necromancer gathered up the money. I pulled from the bottle of spirits I'd brought with me, letting the cold bite into my skin as I gazed at stars and towers of rust, leaning against the rumbling Chrysler as it got warm for Imogen. When the necromancer and the processor reappeared, their masks with their horrible painted eyes saw through me, and I was nothing to them. But I didn't care. The processor put Imogen in the Chrysler, we climbed in and I drove us away, far away from the industrial park and into the dark woods.

I was driving too fast. I was reckless, trembling with fear. The processor unwrapped Imogen. He had stripped her naked and washed her body, cleaned off the soot, so that now the savage burns in all their rawness screamed from what should have been her milk-white skin. Watching in the rear-view mirror, I cried out when I saw her, and began to weep.

The necromancer recited his cryptic words with the same mechanical murmur as he always did, directing the processor, weaving his science of life and death. He had taken with him the skull from my treasure box, my skull, and held it in his lap, idly caressing its crown while he intoned his Medieval secrets. Was he working harder, more earnestly, because he knew I loved this woman? I doubt it, because I perceived him as a monster, but it seemed that perhaps indeed he cared.

As always the processor opened the subject's—Imogen's—abdomen and chest, and removed her liver and kidneys, reaching up beneath the sternum to draw out her heart, and placed them in the tray with the other organs whose names I didn't know. And as always, he carved them with his implements, inscribing them with sigils or magic words before replacing them in Imogen's body and sewing up the wound.

Trees rushed past us, naked in the terror of the headlights.

And then the final part. The processor brought the bottle to her slack, blistered lips and poured the spirits into her throat. And the necromancer said his final words:

"And now she has become real."

I had driven too far out. I wasn't familiar with this stretch of road. And it was getting late, dawn would be coming soon. I turned around and sped back the other way, tearing dirt and gravel into the air behind us. For whatever reason, I knew we had to get back to the laboratory before sunrise.

I was done crying. I'd wiped the tears and snot from my face with the sleeve of my shirt. Now, as I drove us down the road, with the processor sitting quietly on the floor behind me, and the necromancer still idly stroking the crown of that skull, my skull, as he stared (vacantly? Or with deep absorption?) at the body of Imogen, I said, what happens now? Will she live? And the necromancer replied:

"Come with us to the rooftop and see for yourself."

At the industrial park the sky was turning blue with the approaching sun. For the first time, I saw the processor rush, throwing Imogen over his shoulder and racing into the laboratory. The necromancer led me inside for the first time, and I averted my gaze from the steel surgical tables, I refused to glance at the labels on the shelves of plastic bins, my eyes did not linger on the tall translucent vats filled with human bodies suspended in viscous blue. Ascending a metal stairway, we emerged on the roof as the first dawn light was breaking in the east.

The processor had placed Imogen's body on a mat, and now was lighting incense, and now was throwing pink rose petals all around her.

The necromancer touched my arm, holding me at a distance as I watched the proceedings.

Having covered the ground and her body with flowers, the processor stood back, and from the necromancer's valise he retrieved a customized clarinet, and as the red sun broke over the ruins of the cannery and the abandoned factories and warehouses, he began to play a sweet and mystic drone.

Imogen rose from the ground, naked and apparently alive. Amid the smoke and flowers, in the dawn light, she began to dance, swaying her hips, stretching out her arms, undulating her body in a slow, grotesque jazz.

I stepped forward, toward Imogen, toward the sun. The light bathed her in ugliness. She danced in death, her repulsive disfiguration.

And I loved her.

I AM LOOKING FOR A VERY SPECIFIC VIDEO

I am looking for a very specific video.

No, not the one you're thinking of. Not that one either. I doubt you've ever seen it. In fact I doubt I've even seen it—it may have been a dream, or a false memory pieced together from stray images in the back of my mind.

It's possible, perhaps even likely when one considers the details of this rare video, that I unconsciously invented or dreamed its existence, or that perhaps what I once saw has been grossly distorted by my addled memory and overactive imagination. But though the reality or unreality of the video remains an open question, and its existence is perhaps only a slim possibility, nevertheless I am compelled to seek it out until I have either found it or proven once and for all that it cannot be found. Because this latter option (proving nonexistence) may be impossible, my search may go on interminably. While I may set the matter aside from time to time when I grow weary of looking, I will always come back to it sooner or later. While by this point all traces of the video may have been wiped from the face of the earth, if it ever existed at all, it is not conceivable that it could ever be erased from my memory.

I am looking for a very specific video. When I first said these words to you your immediate response was to ask the obvious questions. What kind of video is it? Where did I see it? What happens? What's it about?

I realize my inability to answer these questions must be frustrating, but please don't chalk it up to some childish, stubborn impulse to be mysterious, to create a false aura around myself and around the video. That's really not the case. The fact is I can't answer these questions simply because I don't know how. As difficult as this may be for you to understand, I'm not sure these questions have answers at all. All I can say is that I'm looking for a very specific video, and if you'd seen it I think you'd know.

I am looking for a very specific video. I say these words, and sometimes someone's ears will perk up. They bristle, the hair standing up on their arms and the back of their neck, their spine suddenly stiffening. What have I done to them? What memories have I provoked? What video, real or imagined, is now playing out in their mind's eye? Could it be the same one I'm looking for? I'd like to think so, but the truth is, this is highly unlikely. Sure enough, when I examine their reaction closely, it becomes clear they are thinking of something else entirely.

Though the video I am looking for is difficult to describe, that is not because it is a vague concept, open category, genre, or *kind* of video. I am not looking for something similar. I am looking for a *very specific* video. But though I cannot describe it, it is nevertheless possible to determine what video someone is thinking of by talking with them.

In the expression on their face, in the duration and distance of their haunted gaze, the fidgeting of their fingers, the twitching of their smile and of their eyes—here is where the video is described. If one reads these signs carefully enough, it becomes possible to determine whether or not someone is thinking of the same, specific video. Invariably, and unsurprisingly, they are not.

Why am I looking for this video? What's the point? It all must seem like a game or a prank to you, to someone who has not seen this very specific video. But if you had seen it, or if you had imagined you'd seen it; if there were any glimmer of a memory, even just a single frame or a thumbnail from this video, then you would never ask this question, "why." It would be entirely clear to you why someone like me, someone with a memory of this video, would look for it again. But because you have not seen it, I can scarcely explain things further.

So what would I do if I ever found it again, this very specific video? To tell you the truth, I don't think I'd watch it. I'm not sure that I could handle it—and besides, I wouldn't want to spoil the image of it in my mind, the memory which is possibly more powerful than the video itself. I wouldn't want to watch it, but I'd want to show it to a friend.

I wouldn't share the video with just anyone. I wouldn't post it on social media for everyone to see. A close friend, someone I could trust, someone who trusted me, someone like you—that's who I would share the video with.

I'd hang out with this special friend of mine, perhaps we'd have a couple of drinks, and then casually I'd mention the video. "I'd like to show you something," I'd say slyly, with an odd sparkle in my eyes. "I think you'll like it." And I'd set up the video on my computer, and sit them down on the chair in front of the screen.

"You won't mind if I look away, would you?" I'd say, as I prepare to press the 'play' button. "I've already seen it, you understand, a long time ago. I lost it for a long time, but now I've found it again, and I want to share it with you. Are you ready? Watch carefully. I want you to remember everything."

XIBALBA®

As a child I was never encouraged to do anything in particular—sports, reading, music—nor was I especially discouraged from doing anything else. My parents mostly did not take much of an interest in my upbringing, though there were exceptions, of course. I remember as a small child being taken for swimming "lessons," where without any instruction the "teacher" forced me to jump into a swimming pool and try my best not to drown. In addition to instilling in me a lifelong terror of water, and a total mistrust of all "teachers," this episode taught me another important lesson: no one was ever going to help me do anything. From here on out it was sink or swim, quite literally.

There was another, and much more significant, exception to the general neglect with which I was treated by my parents and the broader society. There was one particular thing that was stressed to me, over and over again, by my parents, by puppets on television, by the advertisements at the beginning of my favorite arcade game, by the police officers who occasionally visited my classrooms, that I was never, under any circumstances, to do: drugs.

It should come as no surprise then, that this injunction—the only real kind of encouragement or direction I ever received from grown-ups or figures of authority, despite it being of a negative and prohibitive nature—became an object of curiosity, gradually evolving into a hobby, a passion, and eventually a single-minded obsession.

I should clarify, it was drugs themselves, not the prohibition of drugs, with which I became fascinated. It began with the bizarre cartoon I was shown as a small child in school, in which marijuana, LSD, and cocaine were personified as freakish, demonic entities seducing victims with promises of pleasure, visions, and magic powers. Though this film, presumably, was intended to frighten us, it had the complete opposite effect. I was enchanted.

The flagrant lies of the teachers and police about the supposed ill effects of illicit substances, easily disproved by a child's internet research, further solidified my belief that there was indeed something powerful and secret that society was conspiring to hide from me. And then came the songs and the novels, Jack Kerouac and rock and roll, all the stuff that young boys are attracted to, all filled with subtle references or explicit endorsements of smoking, snorting, and shooting up. I was hooked, so to speak, before I had ever even tried it.

Lucky for me, as it turned out I was unusually sensitive to the effects of psychotropic substances. At least, at one time I considered this lucky, because it guaranteed I could experience the visionary delights of a drug with less of it on hand (which in my younger days was always the case, money and drugs being hard to come by). In retrospect

I consider my natural sensitivity to hallucination to be anything but fortuitous. These days I regard hallucination as something to be avoided, or suppressed with a double martini. But I'm getting ahead of myself.

My early use of pot, tobacco, and alcohol is hardly interesting and not worth the trouble of recounting. Even my later period of experimentation with psychedelic and dissociative drugs—LSD, psylocibin, MDMA, DXM, ketamine—was probably not that unusual, and though some of the memories from those years could possibly supply enough vignettes to piece together a halfhearted comic *Bildungsroman*, I have no desire to write such a book. Because anyway, all the psychedelic adventures of my teenage years, even those trips which at the time I experienced as transcendental and mystical, life-changing revelations, all of it now seems trivial, delusional, a cruel and elaborate joke, just as devoid of interest and meaning as everything else—it's impossible to feel otherwise now that I've seen Xibalba.

Somewhere in the rainforests of Central America there exists an isolated indigenous tribe who were, until recently, the only human beings on earth with knowledge of an extremely rare and nearly extinct species of ant.

I say this tribe is isolated, but these days what does that mean? They doubtless wear rubber sandals made in Vietnam, t-shirts made in India, and are in possession of, or at least have access to, radio, evangelical Christianity, plastic cutlery, and vaccines. They're just as much part of modernity as we are in the wealthy metropolitan cities—

perhaps more so, precisely because of their struggle against it. They live on the frontiers of the apocalypse that one day will sweep every corner of this planet. When all is said and done, perhaps this is the truest and most fundamental experience of modern reality—the struggle of life and death, the struggle of human beings to defend their land from machetes and flamethrowers, to prevent forests from being annihilated to make way for soybean plantations and oil pipelines.

As I said, this particular tribe, whose name I do not know, were until recently the only human beings with knowledge of a very particular species of ant, now known as the Xibalba ant, *Mortis xibalbiensis*. These days the Xibalba ant is well known, but it was not the tribe who decided to share the existence of the species with the world. On the contrary, the Xibalba ant occupied a secretive and magical place in their communal life, playing a role in certain rituals which would only be profaned by exposure to the vulgar and corrupt science of the decaying urban civilization. More than anything else, I'm sure these people wished to be left alone, except to trade for those few particular commodities that are of use to them, or to seek out medical or legal counsel to defend themselves from the incursions of modern disease and "development."

No, it was the Xibalba ant which was sought out by the city-dwellers. It was Neumann-Winter, Inc., the world's largest and most powerful manufacturer of pharmaceutical drugs, which went searching for this very special insect.

They weren't searching for the Xibalba ant in particular, of course—not at first. Neumann-Winter, along with their competitors, were simply searching for whatever they could find—plants, fungus, even insects or reptiles—anything that had potential for "medical use." The notion of "medical use," as anyone with experience of modern pharmaceuticals will know, is a highly elastic one. When medical use does not exist for a drug, its manufacturer will simply invent a new disease for which their useless (or indeed, possibly quite poisonous) product is then offered as the cure. What Neumann-Winter were really after were not necessarily "medical uses," but simply drugs. Any drugs. Any substance which had any narcotic or stimulant effect on the human body, anything which acted upon the nerves or the tissues, anything which altered the body's delicate balance of chemicals, and which could therefore be marketed as the antidote to one of the endless ailments afflicting their morbidly depressed, diseased, and distracted customers.

Neumann-Winter, Inc. invested billions in state-of-the-art laboratories where chemicals were synthesized, refined, and modified in endless combinations. But they learned over time that the results of these experiments were rarely as profitable as the treasures awaiting them in the world's dwindling rainforests, home to an unfathomable diversity of life—flowers and fruits and venomous snakes, all producing countless thousands of unknown organic compounds in their flesh and skin and organs.

And so Neumann-Winter employed researchers to travel to the most remote indigenous communities, where ancient forms of science passed down through the generations an encyclopedic knowledge of the surrounding ecosystem and the medical, culinary, recreational, religious, and military properties of its many plant and animal species.

Identifying these species, the researchers from Neumann-Winter (or one of its competitors) would take it back to their laboratory to be analyzed, refined, and if possible, turned into a marketable commodity. The millions in profits resulting from this process would of course never find their way back to the people who supplied the knowledge in the first place. It was a much more subtle and sophisticated kind of extraction than the more brutal style of colonial plunder where minerals or agricultural goods were concerned, but it followed the same pattern nonetheless.

It was in this manner that *Mortis xibalbiensis*, the ant with a mysteriously powerful narcotic venom known as xibalbaline, was discovered by Neumann-Winter, Inc., leading to the eventual creation and marketing of the controversial psychiatric drug Xibalba®. But the acquisition of *xibalbiensis*, or more precisely the acquisition of the *knowledge* of the ant, did not come easily. As I have already indicated, the tribe whose name I do not know, who until recently were the only human beings with knowledge of the ant in question, had no desire to divulge the secret of its existence to anyone, especially not the representatives of a foreign multinational corporation, who they knew both from rumor and experience were typically agents of theft and terror, not to be trusted with secrets. It was, rather, the long and patient efforts of an anthropologist, studying the tribe for purely academic purposes, who uncovered the secret of the ant and its role in tribal life—or, more precisely, death.

I was in college when I first tried Xibalba®. I didn't have a prescription, of course—I'd never seen a psychiatrist in my life. But during my time in university, there was a major upsurge among the youth of a new psychiatric diagnosis: Social Collapse Anxiety Disorder, or SCAD. Crippling sensations of impending doom, an undercurrent of dread punctuated by crises of acute and totally debilitating fear, often accompanied by prophetic dreams and visions—all of it brought on by the news stories, more and more frequent with each passing year, of apocalyptic storms, mass shootings, famines, floods, revolutions, and wars. SCAD became so widespread among the youth ages 12-26 that it was practically an epidemic. Moreover, it proved strangely resilient to all extant psychiatric treatment—counseling, art therapy, the whole gamut of pills and injections were tried, with no discernible effect.

It was at this time that the xibalbaline compound was identified by Neumann-Winter, and through clinical trials it was determined that Xibalba® was far beyond an effective treatment for SCAD—by all appearances, it was a miraculous cure.

The youth suffering from Social Collapse Anxiety Disorder, a number of patients which rapidly grew from thousands, to tens, to hundreds of thousands, were prescribed Xibalba® en masse. The results were stunning, but whether or not they could be considered wholly positive was a matter of intense public controversy.

Within days of starting a daily intake of the drug, patients became less depressed, less lethargic, less prone to panic attacks, hallucinations, and bouts of weeping. Within two weeks, a dramatic transformation of the patient's entire personality was apparent. Where before there were tears and screams, laughter and singing could be heard. Where before they suffered alone, now they gathered with friends, drawn especially to others who were taking the same prescription. Tests measuring positive mood and well-being showed scores through the roof, indeed far above what was normal. Patients shed their baggy sweaters and began to dress more confidently—though with an odd predilection for black. There were, also, the small minority of patients that reacted negatively to the drug, sometimes with total psychic breakdown, requiring hospitalization. In some cases, the patients never recovered. But this was rare.

The attraction to black clothing was mirrored in other dark and macabre fascinations, which those on a daily dose of Xibalba® invariably developed. Horror movies and abrasive noise music were the least worrying among these grisly new obsessions. What disturbed parents and doctors much more was the way in which the patients, who before had to avoid all news stories concerning ecological and civilizational decay for fear of triggering their morbid symptoms, now sought out such stories, and seemed to relish in them, clipping the headlines from newspapers, watching the television reports with wide-eyed glee, laughing and joking about terrorist attacks, assassinations, hurricanes, and wildfires. What before filled them with crippling dread was now a source of pure joy. They began to collect odd tokens of death, like animal bones and debris from house fires. Many developed a keen interest in insects, especially those necrophagic species which survived from feasting on dead and decaying animals—maggots, wasps, beetles, and above all, ants. Some patients in college became so obsessed with insects they completely changed their course of study, suddenly dropping computer engineering or art history to pursue entomology.

As for the nightmares, they were not canceled out by the narcotic, but by all accounts actually increased in frequency and intensity. But to the patients taking Xibalba®, these visions of doom were no longer a cause of terror and sleepless nights, but on the contrary a wellspring of secret pleasure and exhilaration. Xibalba®-eaters awoke from long nights of vivid dreaming perfectly well-rested and refreshed, wearing smiles of peace and wisdom far beyond their years. But above all else, the most disturbing manifestation of the psychic changes wrought by Xibalba® were the Death Dances.

It was never clearly understood how or where the Death Dances began, but it was widely agreed-upon that the idea must have spread through the internet, though whatever secret channels were used to promote the trend have never been discovered. Though there's no evidence that the practice spread online, it is the only rational explanation for the phenomenon. The alternative—that thousands of patients taking Xibalba®, spread out across hundreds of towns and cities, all spontaneously were compelled by some instinctual urge to visit cemeteries at night, to dance and wail in a bizarre ritualistic trance—was so unsettling to contemplate that it was rarely even spoken aloud, despite the evidence that seemed to indicate it was the truth.

Youths, slipping out of their homes to congregate at midnight at local cemeteries, swayed and twirled, waltzing with one another to the beat of homemade drums, laughing and shrieking with unwholesome delight. They brought their collections of dead things, their muskrat skulls and bundles of dead flowers, and placed these on makeshift altars (tree stumps, or marble tombs) along with pet insects—huge centipedes, and jars full of squirming white larvae. The patients rarely spoke to one another at these gatherings, but rather, overcome by some collective impulse, gave themselves over completely to dancing, or to gazing at the ghastly altar, or sometimes just to sleeping in the dirt, wrapped in nightmares, among their raving friends.

When the chilling screams of the dancers alerted the police, or some parent came upon the shocking scene while searching for their missing child, the meeting would be shut down, and scandalous reports would appear in the next morning's newspaper. Such stories could be found in dozens of local newspapers across the country within the span of the first few weeks after Xibalba® began to be prescribed. A similar pattern followed the breakup of the initial congregations—the youths, as if drawn by some inner compass like migratory birds, crept away from their homes and into the woods, or the desert, or the parking lots of abandoned shopping malls, whatever patches of darkness and mystery they could find, and there they found one another, and enacted their *Danse Macabre* once again, sans graves.

As the stories of these nocturnal gatherings were picked up by the national press, it became more and more clear that the Xibalba®-eaters could not be dissuaded from their desire to dance. When prevented from attending this bizarre black mass, patients became sullen and despondent, almost as if the symptoms of the dreaded SCAD were returning. Fearing relapse, parents became reluctant to deny their children this apparently harmless, albeit undoubtedly creepy, recreation. Leading psychiatrists weighed in, and many of them—especially those with a special relationship to Neumann-Winter, Inc., who were eager to suppress any moral panic about the mass drugging of the youth—declared that the patients should be allowed to dance.

There was no question that the gruesome fascinations of the Xibalba®-eaters, the apparent delight they took in destruction and decay, and above all their grotesque nocturnal promenades, were unsettling in the extreme. But who could argue with the dramatic decline of suicide rates and violent behavior? The improved grades, the smiles, the laughter, the virtual disappearance of gloom and anxiety? Though they could and would meet anywhere, the patients expressed an overwhelming preference for the cemetery for their ghastly festivities, and, unless it were guarded by the police, they would always try to meet in a graveyard. And why not? After all, the dancers never defaced the graves, but treated the dead and their monuments with the utmost respect. Why shouldn't they be allowed to dance?

In the midst of the Death Dance controversy, some parents attempted to take their children off of Xibalba®—with disastrous results. As it turned out, the withdrawal symptoms incurred by ceasing intake of the drug were even worse than the disease it was intended to cure. The symptoms of SCAD returned with a tenfold vengeance. It was hypothesized that the patients, while taking the drug, had come to accept certain facts, to embrace certain truths about life and about the Earth and about the future, which no sober mind could possibly integrate. Without Xibalba®, these insights, these new thresholds of understanding, became impossible for the mind to sustain, and the result was often fatal.

As for Neumann-Winter, they were reaping hundreds of millions in profits. One may even be justified in imagining that they had engineered the apocalypse just to provoke Social Collapse Anxiety Disorder and sell Xibalba®. Marshaling their vast public relations expertise, they turned the tide of public debate in favor of the drug. Despite the shock, the moral denunciations, the conspiracy theories, sales only went up and up.

The Death Dance scandal prompted greater public scrutiny of Xibalba®, and soon afterward a detailed investigation into the drug appeared in a leading magazine. It was here that I first learned about *Mortis xibalbiensis*, the Xibalba ant. Apparently, at a Neumann-Winter production facility in Bangalore there was a massive underground ant farm where the insects were bred. For whatever reason, the expert chemists at Neumann-Winter were totally unable to synthesize the xibalbaline compound, and so it had to be produced "naturally." The ants were raised in huge vats filled with synthetic dirt, and their venom harvested the most efficient way possible—by washing and pulverizing the ants, blending them into a paste, then chemically extracting the xibalbaline.

There was nothing in the article about the origins of the Xibalba ant, just a short parenthetical note indicating it had been "discovered" in Central America. It was only later that I learned the details of the insects' origins, at which time it became obvious why Neumann-Winter was keen on keeping these facts out of public view.

As prescriptions of Xibalba® skyrocketed, it became inevitable that the drug would be abused. In the online drug forums I frequented—populated by rogue chemists, amateur shamans, and people like me who were simply obsessed with the mystique and the thrill of drugs—stories about recreational abuse of xibalbaline began to circulate.

The initial reports were highly mixed. Some spoke of revelatory emotional insights accompanied by intense euphoria. Others told of a harrowing descent into cold, desolate basements of the psyche. What united all the experiences was a subtle but profound shift in perception, which the writers of the reports struggled to put into words, but which seemed to be a more brief, intense, concentrated version of the psychic change wrought on prescription Xibalba®-eaters.

The preferred method for a xibalbaline trip was insufflation—crushing the black Xibalba® pills into a fine powder and snorting it. As I said, I was in university at this time, and knew several people who had been prescribed the drug. The stuff was everywhere, and it was easy to get my hands on a few pills.

My first line of the black powder did not give me any pleasure. I didn't feel anything, except for a chilling, electric sensation in my bones and skin, that was neither painful nor pleasant. What was most striking about the experience was not any physical sensation, but a change in consciousness. It was like I saw everything, the world in its entirety, stripped, absurd, and yet whole for the first time.

I did another line, and then another.

The astute reader will have recognized the word Xibalba as the name of the Maya underworld. Strictly speaking, the tribe who were the guardians of the *Mortis xibalbiensis* were not Maya, but their culture, though highly isolated and idiosyncratic, was infused with Maya language and myth. Though their vision of the underworld differed radically from that recorded in the major source of Maya mythology, the *Popol Vuh*, for whatever reason they appropriated the name, passing it along to the Xibalba ant, and thus to Neumann-Winter, Inc.'s Xibalba®.

The anthropologist who was the first outsider to witness the ceremonies has since disappeared, and her research remains unpublished. According to certain theories that circulated online, this was no coincidence— the details of the tribe's funerary practices were now a proprietary secret of Neumann-Winter, Inc.

It was speculated that Neumann-Winter, in addition to sending its own researchers to the last remaining vestiges of free culture and wild nature in search of profitable chemicals, conducted illegal surveillance of anthropologists, botanists, and other scientists working in the rainforest. When anything from this ostensibly academic, not-for-profit research looked promising, Neumann-Winter did whatever they needed to do to obtain it.

I sincerely wish that I knew the details of the secret rites involving the Xibalba ant, but everything I know is pieced together from rumors, guesswork, and the findings of amateur investigators. It was said that the ants, believed by the tribe who guarded them to be servants of the God of Death, were ritualistically eaten by shamans to commune with the god and receive visions. The consumption of xibalbaline by the tribe was carefully regulated. It was understood that the drug was immensely powerful and should only be used in minute quantities, in order to steal glances behind the curtain, not to be overwhelmed with visions but only to be gently reminded—of something. It was certainly never administered to children.

The ants were said to dwell in certain sacred fields, in towering cities of black clay. When members of the tribe passed away, their bodies were brought to the secret fields and laid down amid the anthills. *Mortis xibalbiensis* would come, then, in their fervent millions, to strip all flesh and tissue from the corpses, until only bones were left. Skeletal remains, picked clean, littered the earth between the insect mounds.

While the ants feasted, a man would remain, armed with a spear or a rifle, to protect the body from vultures and jaguars. It was critical that only the ants, and no other creatures, were allowed to carry off the flesh of the dead because, it was believed, the ants were transporting the deceased, bit by bit, to Xibalba.

In my experiments snorting the crushed Xibalba® pills, I found myself constantly on the edge of a black dawn that would not break. Something was there, just beyond my reach, and I wanted it badly. It wasn't just that I wanted to be the first person to have attained some new plateau of the drug's effects, so that I could brag about it to my friends and to my fellow psychotropic hobbyists online. It was much more than that. My instincts told me there was something more to this mysterious substance which had seemed to have taken our culture hostage almost over night, and wrought such striking and bizarre transformations on its habitual users. I wanted to penetrate its secrets.

It occurred to me that by breaking the xibalbaline hydrochloride down into its free base form (a relatively simple chemical process called trituration, the same used to make crack out of cocaine), I may be able to achieve a more intense, albeit briefer, trip, by smoking the drug. From what I could find on the internet, no one else had attempted this yet, but from my understanding of the drug's chemistry it was completely possible.

During the prior week of experimentation, I found myself afflicted by extreme mood swings, alternating between violent attacks of anxiety and long hours of placid bliss in which I stared in silent meditation at videos of eagles feasting on roadkill or time-lapse photography of decomposing trees. I craved the black powder, and struggled to limit my intake of it. I admit it's possible that my decision to manufacture its more powerful, crystallized form was due in part not merely to my curiosity, but to my urge to consume ever larger and more potent doses of the chemical.

Finally, I was able to acquire an entire small jar of the pills, which it seemed with each passing week were flooding the streets in ever greater volumes. I crushed the pills and triturated the powder in my apartment kitchen, obtaining a quantity of dull black crystal. I locked myself in my bedroom, and smoked it.

Why was it so difficult to gather information about the origins of Xibalba®? For one, Neumann-Winter, Inc. didn't want their competitors replicating the drug, and cutting in to the record-breaking profits which they reaped from its sales. But there was another reason. If certain details about the drug's production were widely known, it perhaps would have been unlikely that anyone would have been able to stomach the pills, whatever their apparent benefits.

Neumann-Winter tried, and failed, to synthesize xibalbaline once they had isolated the compound. It proved impossible to manufacture in a lab. But supposedly, when they tried raising the Xibalba ant under controlled conditions, this also resulted in failure. The drug remained elusive, until one of the chemists, in reviewing the secret files on the Xibalba ant, realized the problem might be in the insects' diet.

They'd been feeding the ants offal and slaughterhouse byproducts, but this wouldn't do. They had to replicate much more precisely the diet of those funerary anthills in the distant rainforest. According to whispered rumors, this is exactly what Neumann-Winter did, and continued to do, in the secret production facility in Bangalore. How, where, and from whom they obtained and still continue to obtain the ghoulish fodder is a matter of speculation, but the basic facts seem clear enough. The workers, technicians, chemists, and guards who work in the ant farm underground at the lab are forced to sign non-disclosure agreements promising to never reveal what they've seen. Nevertheless, several have come forward (anonymously, online) who claim to have seen with their own eyes this vast cthonic banquet of death, streaming with millions of ants.

When I smoked the black crystal I saw things which I shall never repeat to a living soul. I witnessed things, I *came to understand* things, which I shall never forget, but that I shall take to my grave where they belong.

I suppose it may only have been fifteen minutes, give or take, that I was in the shadows, though it felt like hours, or days.

While I was there, while I was in Xibalba, the City of Death (for indeed, that is where I was), I was not afraid. Though I saw dreadful things, I understood them with perfect clarity, I sympathized and even rejoiced in them, and so I could not be afraid. I journeyed through Xibalba and I was one with it.

Towers of clay and black crystal reared in fiery subterranean skies, an architecture of blind malevolence, like termite mounds or ant hills. Dizzy with its own absurdity, the city loomed and sparkled, towering over a vast darkness. I was shown secret images, secret words were whispered in my ears—things I cannot repeat, and which ever since I have tried to forget.

It was not hell. There was no punishment here. It was something much worse. It was not death, but life, our life. It was not the underworld, but a vision of the earth which at last I could perceive in brutal, ecstatic clarity. It was not another dimension, but our dimension, a vast, entropic field, decaying and giving life to some sweeping unconscious Will. Creation and destruction, architecture and war, nature and imagination—I now perceived the stark unity of all things as a terrible banquet, consuming and being consumed by the entire universe. And I was not afraid.

It was only afterward, when the effects of the drug began to subside, and I slowly began to adjust to the cold light of my bedroom, that I began to panic. And I suppose that panic has never really gone away, as much as I've tried to suppress it with alcohol and sedatives.

I flushed the remnants of the black crystal down the toilet and swore to never touch the stuff again. But with each day that I am haunted by the memory of what I saw, which I am reminded of by every news report of riots, storms, bombings, food shortages, and sober predictions of how everything in the world would only get worse and worse and worse, with each day that goes by I'm less sure that I'll be able to keep this promise.

More and more people are taking Xibalba®. Not just the youth, and not just the especially depressed and mentally diseased populations of the overfed nations. All demographics, all over the world, more and more, are going to the doctor with complaints of anxiety, panic, depression, insomnia, and all the other symptoms of Social Collapse Anxiety Disorder. And who could blame them? It's impossible not to be effected by what's happening to the world, and when one is suffering, it's only reasonable to ask for medicine. And for this disease, there is no better medicine than Xibalba®.

I swore never to take it again, but perhaps this was a foolish pledge to make. After all, there's no reason why I have to abuse the stuff. My adventurous days are behind me. I don't want to get high anymore. I just want to be at peace with myself, with my memories, and with everything that's happening in the world.

I know that if I take Xibalba® the terrible things I've seen will not be terrible anymore, but beautiful. And all the horror on television, and outside my window—beautiful.

Perhaps it's what I need. Perhaps it's what we all need, now. A world given over to Xibalba®. A world given over to wasps, millipedes, maggots, worms, dung beetles, and ants.

THE MONARCHS

The house was much larger than I had anticipated. So large, in fact, that its end could not be seen. An unyielding labyrinth of brush and rose thickets blocked one side of the building, and on the other side stretched a vast, unnamed pond. The house, a rambling mass of faded blue clapboards and blackish shingles, grimy windows and tottering turrets, extended back and out toward the distant hills.

The property, christened the Monarchs by its Victorian builder, was now my home. And like the house, my stay had no foreseeable end. I had been ordered by the Radical Axis to resolve certain contradictions in the Revolutionary Design, a project code-named Operation Polarize, and it was decided that I—along with my partner—would reside in the Monarchs for the duration of the struggle. Long since abandoned, the property had recently been requisitioned by the Radical Axis. Owing to its exquisite observatory, it was deemed an ideal location for this top-secret operation.

I arrived in the afternoon, dropped off by a Radical cadre who promptly turned the car around and left me alone as soon as I shut the car door. Venturing through the heavy front doors of the Monarchs, I discovered a large drawing room near the front of the house, and there set up my camp near the fireplace.

The property, it was said, was named after the migratory monarch butterflies which in former times sought refuge in the trees of the garden. Arriving in their thousands, they clustered on the branches of trees like barnacles of the air. Now that the butterfly is extinct, I suppose the word 'monarch' has lost some of its delicacy. Children in the future will think only of dusty queens, jealous wars, armies, a history of pettiness and blood.

The next day, my partner arrived. He was a diminutive man with a ponytail, shaggy sideburns, and a thin mustache. According to my dossier he was one of the leading lights of the Radical movement, though I'd never heard of him until now. Apparently he pioneered a new science which finally reconciled Ptolemaic astrology with quantum astrophysics, a breakthrough with major implications for the Revolution. He arrived in the afternoon, driven in a car followed by a pickup truck loaded with crates of supplies. Cadres in blue uniforms unloaded the crates into the Monarchs while I introduced myself to the young stargazer, Cadre Number 48225 *nom de guerre* Fritz.

Fresh and eager, Fritz greeted me in the conventional way by first saluting and then hugging me, and calling me "Comrade." I did not have to fake enthusiasm for his arrival, for the supplies were indeed a major relief to my nerves. There was plenty of food and coffee, a whole crate of the books I had requested, blankets, clothes, everything that could be desired.

Fritz insisted right away on showing me his virtual reality headset, which was state of the art and programmed with all the latest simulations. I had to assure him repeatedly that I would try it out.

"What's the local bar scene?" he said abruptly.

"Pardon me?"

"The bars, the bars—don't tell me you haven't looked in on it yet."

I scratched my chin. "I'm not so sure about the locals, comrade. I think we ought to drink here at the Monarchs."

Fritz gave me a look of mild disgust.

"We'll look into it," he replied. "Don't you worry." He slapped me on the back and gave my shoulder a squeeze, like I had told him my wife had just left me, or that I'd been diagnosed with a non-fatal but nevertheless unpleasant disease.

The cadres finished unloading the supplies, and one of them stood waiting with a clipboard for me to sign. As soon as I gave him my signature, they were off, turning round in the driveway loop and heading back down the dirt road away from the Monarchs.

Fritz wanted to check out the local bars, but this was out of the question. We had been expressly ordered to avoid all contact with the local population. Apparently, the Monarchs were widely believed to be cursed. The locals feared the place, and strongly disproved of the Radicals moving in to occupy it. This was just as well for all I was concerned. I had no wish to mix with strange people. I was here to work, and if I needed to blow off steam I could take a stroll in the abandoned gardens. Anyway, the Radical Axis had doubtless stationed cadres undercover in the village to keep tabs on us. Fritz must have known all this, but I suppose he had a different attitude to things than I did.

That night Fritz and I ate and drank gin in the dusty drawing room by the fire, swapping stories about our work and our time with the Radical Axis. Fritz kept me up late with his stories and games, but it's important to get comfortable with someone if you're going to be working closely together and sharing quarters. And so I overslept the next morning, didn't get to my early morning work, but that was fine.

I slept on an antique red-cushioned sofa, the ornately carved wood all painted with gold, which I had dragged close to the fire. Fritz slept across from me on a matching chair and ottoman, an Axis-issue blanket draped over his lap, his head lolled to the side with his mouth open, snoring loudly all through the night. In the morning we boiled water for coffee and cooked some bacon. Afterward I shaved and bathed in the freezing-cold pond, but when I returned inside I found Fritz still in the drawing room, sitting in his armchair wearing his virtual reality headset.

Hearing me come in, he removed it and began insisting that I try it on. When I politely declined, explaining there was much work to be done, he shook his head knowingly and returned to his games. It was not until late in the morning, practically midday, that he was ready to work. By that time I'd already finished organizing my books and notes, set up my word processor, and typed several pages of my reflections addressing the contradictions of the Revolutionary Design. I was making another cup of coffee and slicing myself a piece of bread when Fritz emerged from his virtual stupor, asked for coffee, and requested that I show him the way to the observatory.

Fritz was wearing a pair of tight denim trousers and nothing else. His hands shoved into his pockets, his knees slightly bent, his curly hair tucked behind his ears, he frowned at me vacantly while I took a meaningful chew of my buttered slice. I didn't necessarily care that he had wasted his entire morning. What irked me was this infantile way of asking me to take him to the observatory. I wasn't in charge. I didn't know anything about the observatory or anything else related to his job.

"I don't know where it is," I told him plainly. "But I saw it from outside. Perhaps we can find it together."

We strolled with our hot mugs of coffee down the dark and dusty passages of the Monarchs for some time, taking with us an electric lantern to light the way. Fritz had slipped on some sandals to avoid stabbing his bare feet on splintered wood or ancient nails, and they made an unpleasant slapping noise with every step.

I had seen the dome and the protruding telescope, pointed in the direction of the lake, from outside the building, and so I was able to guess how to reach it from within. After a couple of wrong turns and incorrect doors leading to empty ballrooms and disused closets, we discovered it. It was the only room in the house which had been refurbished by Radical operatives before our visit. Or, more precisely, the telescope itself had been refurbished. The vast, antique arsenal of beaten copper domes and glinting shafts had been repaired and polished, so that now it gleamed in the sunlight pouring in from the aperture in the domed roof through which the telescope protruded. Other than the telescope itself, nothing in the room had been repaired or cleaned; a film of cobwebs and dust covered the supercomputers and the desks, and the paintings that hung lopsided on the wall were coated in gray filth.

I asked Fritz dryly if he would be able to find his way back, and he assured me he'd be fine. Explaining I had much work to do, I left him there, with his hands shoved in the pockets of his pants, just staring at the telescope.

As I navigated the corridors back toward my makeshift office, at some point I must have taken a wrong turn. For I came through a door and found myself in a dusty sitting room. The windows, overlooking the garden, had been smashed by some ancient storm or vandal, but otherwise the room was eerily pleasant. Still with half my cup of coffee to finish, I walked to the broken windows, where dead leaves and detritus had blown in to cover the floor, and—after inspecting it for possible shards of broken glass—sat down on an old chair.

Rose brambles sprawled out amid the stout trunks of oak trees. In the old flower beds and pots tall grasses quivered with the movement of rodents. What once might have been a careful plan of hedges and fences was now an unintelligible mess. I realized with some disappointment that walking through it may not be possible or pleasant.

But at least it was fine to gaze at the roses from here, and enjoy the breeze.

Then, as I sipped my coffee, I saw movement. Not another vole, but something white, shining in the gray sun, slipping like a mist between the tangled thorns. Squinting, I tried to make it out, and then it came around from behind a hedgerow—a human body.

I jumped, spilling coffee on my hand and thigh. When I looked again the figure was gone.

Over the next few weeks I returned daily to the sitting room with the broken windows, but I never caught sight of the figure again. Soon I ceased expecting to see anything, but kept coming back out of habit. I had my coffee there each morning, and sometimes I would return at night, but whatever I had seen did not appear again.

That night I was disturbed by a creaking sound, which I had hurt faint hints of on my first night in the Monarchs, but which now was closer, louder, and more frequent. It was never loud enough to wake me, but if I happened to be working late, or drinking with Fritz as he often insisted I do, then I could hear it—the faint groaning of old wood, shrinking from the breeze coming in off the pond. And the wind itself, ringing through some breach or cranny in the dilapidated house, hummed and sang in a gross vibrato—a frightful noise, which at night I imagined warbled into the dim approximation of some lost melody.

Ignoring the orders of the Radical Axis, Fritz ventured into the village one night during our first week. He came back drunk, insisting that the locals were perfectly friendly, decent people. He went again, and then again, but on this third night he returned in a furious, deluded state. Unable to sleep, I was typing at my desk when he barged in from the summer night.

"Beastly, these country women," he grumbled, tearing off his shirt and flinging it into the pile in the corner of the room where he stored his clothes. His eyes were red, his face unshaven. He tottered unsteadily from one leg to the other as he poured himself a glass of gin.

I asked him what had happened, and in reply he barked an acidic laugh. "Oh, nothing happened. Nothing. *Nothing!* Just these people, man. Earth women. They're dead inside. If you touch their thighs and their breasts," he added ironically, "you will discover dirt and twigs, and the skulls of raccoons."

I surmised he had been thrown out of the village tavern, and couldn't help but feel relieved that this had happened sooner rather than later. There was only so much work I could do on my own, without the data from Fritz's astronomical research. I had no moral objection to his poor work ethic, it was simply that for both our sake's, to fulfill our duty to the Radical Axis and to the Revolution, and to avoid spending the rest of our lives in the Monarchs, we needed to finish our work, and Fritz was easily distracted. If now he was done with the village, and could renew his commitment to our work, I would be pleased.

Fritz collapsed into his armchair, half-dressed and clutching a glass of gin, and promptly fell asleep with his mouth and eyes hanging open ghoulishly. The wind rang, the chilling vibrato like a child practicing the violin in some dark corner of the wasted house.

"We don't need to return to some deeper way of being, supposedly lost. I don't think we've lost anything. We've abandoned the things we no longer need. There's no sense in hanging on to these old trinkets, or playing with obsolete technology. Let those pathways grow over and return to nature, let it be a wilderness. We don't need those paths anymore. The future is in the stars, my friend."

The next morning, Fritz was transformed. He woke up early, shaved the fluff from his cheeks, washed his hair, and made breakfast and coffee for us both. I was still rubbing the sleep from my eyes—I'd been up writing until close to daybreak—when I awoke to the aromas of coffee and food. While we ate, Fritz went on about the future, astrology, and the Radical movement.

"Once Willow gets here, yes, everything will change. Then I'll have the future in my grasp, and the planets will open up to me like flowers."

"Who's Willow?"

"But I've just explained, weren't you listening? I ordered her this morning, over the phone. She should be arriving in a few weeks. Are you feeling alright? Here, try one of these…"

He extended a hand with a white pill in his palm—I recognized it as a standard Axis-issue productivity drug. So this was the secret of his sudden change. I declined it with a wave of my hand.

"Suit yourself," he said with a disapproving smugness, and then quickly launched back into his talk, which I henceforth completely ignored.

Days and weeks passed and I watched the roses die. I was beginning to feel trapped in the Monarchs, but at least Fritz was working. He didn't give up drinking or virtual reality, and still frequently walked around barefoot and shirtless, scratching his scrawny, hairy chest, but now he spent long hours in the observatory, peering into the black eyeholes attached to the vast telescope, fixing up the computers and making them purr. He supplied me with computer readouts, charts, and calculations, and was patient with my questions as I tried to make sense of them. As for me, I believed I was making progress, but the big questions still bedeviled me. For every step forward I took, fresh complications were raised, and the whole issue seemed intractable. And then the leaves in the garden trees began to turn, the mornings cooled and the little waves of the pond became harsh and icy on the grassy lip of the earth. And still we worked.

When the first red leaves fell to the earth, I discovered them littering a long, coffin-shaped wooden crate which had been deposited on the porch of the Monarchs. It was addressed to Fritz, so I fetched him from the observatory and he raced excitedly out. He found a rusty crowbar in the garden shed and used it to pry open the box. Reaching into the mass of golden straw, he pulled out a lifesize doll in the shape of a woman.

"Willow," he said, not to me but to the doll. "You're finally here."

He brushed the packaging straw off of her painted face and her black dress, and proceeded to drag her into the house. Elsewhere in the Monarchs we had discovered a small white marble-topped table with a decorative wrought-iron base, and matching iron chairs. We used it for eating and drinking coffee. Into one of these chairs Fritz propped up his new doll, assuring her he would only take a moment to make them a fresh cup of coffee, asking if she wanted cream and sugar, quizzing her about her trip and if she'd been comfortable in the wooden crate, etc.

The corner of our chamber where I worked—my "office"—I had set apart with an old Japanese-style paneled screen I'd found in one of the bedrooms, in order to spare myself the distraction of Fritz snoring or enjoying his virtual reality headset while I was trying to work. But now he was talking, chatting and giggling while he had coffee with the doll. I had to plug my ears with cotton balls in order to focus on my work.

I believe Fritz went to the observatory at one point to work on his telescope, but that evening he was back for a candlelit dinner with Willow. He made spaghetti bolognese—I'd never seen him cook before—and didn't even offer any to me, but instead placed a full plate, complete with Parmigiano-Reggiano and large glass of Chianti, in front of the doll.

Willow herself never moved her limbs, never made any sound or gesture, not even the faintest twitch of her plush lips or heavily-lined eyes. She just sat or stood wherever Fritz placed her, staring silently and placidly at nothing. As I grew increasingly annoyed with Fritz's tiresome antics, I inwardly joked that I envied her oblivion.

After dinner—I nicked some of the Parmigiano and Chianti—I tried to get back to work, but the distractions now only worsened. Dragging a gramophone out of some unknown corner, Fritz put on Chubby Checker's rendition of "The Twist." Coaxing Willow from her chair, he began to dance. Having stripped off the button-down he wore for dinner, Fritz was now wearing just his customary denim pants, shirtless and shoeless. Sticking out his elbows, he twisted one foot back and forth on the wood floor, shook his hips, did the twist while Willow stood immobile beside him.

Yes, I could have looked away, but something about it was mesmerizing. After some time I managed to tear my gaze from the unwholesome spectacle and with great effort resumed my work. But soon afterward the evening reached its climax—actually, plateau is a better word, because it went on for countless hours.

Disturbed by the sound of sighs, grunts, and moans, I unplugged my ears and peered around the corner of my dividing screen. There, on a pile of blankets before the fireplace, Fritz had mounted the doll and was feverishly making love to it.

Fritz never exercised. In fact he barely moved all day. Moreover, he drank like a fish. He couldn't possibly be in good physical condition. And yet there he was, furiously humping like a greyhound, for what ended up being several hours, only with small breaks to drink some water, towel the sweat off his face, and rearrange the doll for a different angle. His stamina baffled me. I wondered if he were taking some pills, perhaps something else Axis-issue from the supply crates, and I briefly worried that he'd give himself an aneurysm if he kept up like this. In any case, it was impossible to work or sleep under these circumstances. It was the noise above all else—the creaking of the floorboards, the slapping of flesh against plastic, but especially the cries and obscene phrases uttered at a shameless volume by Fritz—which prevented me from concentrating on anything, even with the cotton balls stuck in my ears. After some time of trying to ignore it, I realized I would have to relocate, perhaps permanently, to another section of the Monarchs.

Fritz paid no heed to me as I packed up my materials into a box and carried it out of the drawing room we'd been sharing. The wind was blowing that night, and as I lugged my things down dark corridors I was caught between the grunts and sighs of Fritz and the eerie drone of the house. The word "spirit" comes from Latin *spiritus*, meaning breath—in a literal sense, the sound was the spirit of the Monarchs. It grew louder as I traversed the corridor toward what I hoped would be my refuge, the room with the broken windows overlooking the garden. Fritz's sighs followed me down the corridors, but finally here, in this place, those sounds faded entirely, drowned out by the haunting drone of the house.

It was more distinct tonight than ever before, the humming wind. Buzzing in the guttural chasms, it choked and hummed, and I almost thought formed certain very old words. Strangely, when I came to the room with broken windows, there was no forceful wind blowing in, only the gentlest breeze which scarcely rocked the boughs of the trees outside. And yet the spirit of the house groaned and sang as if with the gusts of a powerful storm.

I wiped the cobwebs off of a table and chair I found in a nearby room and dragged them in to my new office, setting my lantern onto the dust-covered sideboard. I was able to work, but here, though I was away from Fritz and Willow, I did not yet feel alone. I constantly felt the hair on the back of my neck standing up, and sensed a presence there in the room with me. Eventually I had to turn my writing table around so that my back was to the wall and I could face the door and broken windows. Even this did not alleviate my paranoia completely, as the voice of the house still seemed to whisper in my ear, and I had to constantly look up when I thought I saw something moving in the corner of my eye, which never turned out to be there.

Some time later in the night, stuck on a particularly difficult section of my work, I decided to go on a walk to clear my head. Passing by the drawing room encampment, I stole another piece of cheese, averting my eyes from Fritz's ongoing exertions. I also grabbed a sweater from my box of folded clothing, as the night was getting chilly.

Since the morning, more leaves had fallen from the trees around the Monarchs. As I walked, munching Parmigiano and taking in the crisp air, I found myself heading, perhaps unconsciously at first, in the direction of the village. Until then I had barely laid eyes on it, only glimpsing the outline of the quaint houses and shops in the distance. As I made my way down the road, I saw the golden lights in the windows, and the smoke rising from the chimneys.

Why had the Radical Axis forbidden us from visiting the village? What was here that we were not supposed to see? Strangely, I had not considered these questions until now. But in the cold night they became issues of sudden critical importance. As I wandered closer, I perceived fog and voices rising from a pond on the outskirts of the village. I was astonished to discover that the pond was frozen over, and was being used for ice-skating by the gathered villagers; astonished because it was still early in the autumn, and I was not aware that there had been a frost.

My amazement only deepened as I drew closer to the ice rink, for I realized it was not a pond, but a football field which had been sprayed with water to create ice for skating. It resembled, to a remarkable degree, the football field, encircled by a red clay track, from the small village where I was raised. As a child, I spent many hours walking around that clay track, by myself or with a friend, ruminating and dreaming. The resemblance was so strong that for a brief moment I was nearly convinced that this was in fact the same field, and that I had wandered into the village of my childhood. I quickly dismissed this thought, however, for its clear absurdity—nevertheless, the chilling sense of familiarity remained with me.

Some people were sitting in camp chairs, drinking hot chocolate and chatting. Children and people of all ages skated in circles on the ice, wearing mittens and caps, their scarves fluttering picturesquely behind them. I now understood Fritz's obscure reference to raccoons from his time in the village, for I saw several of the animals skittering about on the ice or sitting in peoples' laps.

As for the skaters, they glided with perfect ease in circles around the ice. It seemed they barely needed to kick or propel themselves; standing upright, they sailed around and around with infinite momentum. Their faces were wooden and gray, frozen in cryptic smiles, their eyes staring blankly ahead.

I was so agog at the scene that I didn't notice the raccoon's approach until it leaped onto my thigh and began scurrying up my midsection. I cried out in terror, but the beast was undeterred—it was after my cheese. Seizing the half-eaten chunk of Parmigiano in its mouth right out of my hand, it kicked off of me and then scurried a few feet away, clutching the cheese in its tiny, primeval hands and nibbling ecstatically.

"Are you okay?"

Giggling, smiling…she was beautiful, not like the wooden faces of the others. She was wearing shorts that exposed her thighs, decorated with tattoos of autumn branches and raccoon skulls just as Fritz had described.

"I'm sorry about your cheese," she said.

"I don't need it," I replied quickly. "I was just…"

What was I doing? Surely not visiting the village, which was expressly forbidden by the Radical Axis. For all I knew, she was a cadre, stationed here to observe my activities. Having trailed off, I gulped as my eyes wandered the scene, casting about for something to say, something to justify my presence. We were some distance from the ice, away from the others. Who was she? Where had she come from? Why had she approached me like this?

"Do you want to skate?" she offered.

"No, no, no. I'd better not. I have to go now."

"You're staying at the Monarchs. You're a Radical."

Flustered, I opened my mouth but no words came out. The woman tilted her head to one side suggestively.

"Let me walk you back," she offered. "I know a shortcut."

Without waiting for a reply, she began to walk, not down the road I'd arrived by, but into the trees which separated the village from the gardens of the Monarchs. I followed behind her in silence, into the darkness. I can't understand how she could find her way, because the woods were completely dark, and any light from within the Monarchs would not be visible from this approach, as the drawing room encampment was on the opposing wing of the house. I could not see her in the tangle of shadows, but I followed the sound of her footsteps on the dry leaves. And then, much sooner than I thought possible, we emerged into the moonlight of the rose garden, the overgrown thickets, bare of flowers or leaves, sprawling out toward the imposing gloom of the Monarchs' unending clapboards and shingles and broken windows.

"Come visit us again," said my guide, and then she faded into the trees and I was left there amid the thorns, directly below the broken windows where my desk and writing materials awaited my return. And the haunting vibrato resounded from the house, from the jagged teeth of the broken windows.

That's when I saw it, for the first time since my initial vision—the flash of white, the movement of that ghostly figure. Running towards it, I stumbled in the darkness and fell face-first on the cold, dirty paving stones. But pushing myself up, I realized it was not a paving stone at all, but a grave marker I had slapped my cheek against. Brushing away the dirt and roots which covered it, I peered in the bright moonlight at the engraving...

Here Lie Eleanor and Josephine Subrosa, Sisters
Beloved by the People

The words hit me with a physical force, like the shock of being suddenly flipped upside down and then brought back down on my feet—though the whole time I remained laying in the dirt, my face just inches from the gravemarker. Blinking dizzily, I read and re-read the engraving, as memories and associations flooded into my mind.

How could I have forgotten? The Monarchs were built by none other than the infamous robber baron, the scientist and fertilizer magnate Heinrich Rosa, whose daughters Eleanor and Josephine (changing their surname to Subrosa to symbolize treason against their elite extraction), were among the most famous, indeed legendary, Radicals of their day, Eleanor the occult philosopher, orator, and physician, and Josephine the novelist. It may seem improbable that I would have forgotten (and that nobody would have reminded me) of details of such historical magnitude, but then again, while the Subrosa Sisters were esteemed, their names and portraits regarded with utmost respect, their actual writings had themselves been mostly forgotten, passed over in favor of others in the Radical tradition deemed to be more relevant for the contemporary conjuncture.

Recovering from the blow of this revelation, I staggered to my feet, only to be confronted by the final and most devastating of the night's strange visions. For standing before me was the figure in white, the phantom I had glimpsed first many nights ago, and now again just moments prior. And seeing her face to face, it was now unmistakable who she was—the oval face, long nose, piercing eyes, the elaborate Victorian coiffure, the dress. The ghost of Eleanor Subrosa said nothing, but I was not prepared to miss this opportunity. I was just about to breach the silence, to speak to her, to ask her the ultimate question, when the sound came—the vibrato drone, ringing out from the house.

Turning, I perceived another figure in white, sitting romantically on the windowsill of a turret just above the broken windows of my chamber, playing a ghostly violin. Though I could not see her clearly, I had no doubt that this was Eleanor's sister, Josephine, who I just now recalled was well-known for her penchant for playing the violin in precisely this fashion.

"You must not be afraid…" said Eleanor.

Turning back round to face her, I clasped my hands together beseechingly. "But everything is so strange these days. It was simpler in your time. Can't you see these are terrifying times?"

"It's never been simple," Josephine called down from the windowsill, setting the violin down in her lap. "You're just a prig."

I looked anxiously at Eleanor to see if she would confirm or rebuke this awful judgment, but she said nothing.

"What you should really do," Josephine went on, "is throw a party at the Monarchs, like in the old days…"

"But I'm not allowed to mix with people from the village. And besides, they're all afraid of the Monarchs. They think it's haunted."

"If you can learn how to speak with ghosts without fear, no door will remain closed to you for long."

I had so many questions to ask the ghosts of Eleanor and Josephine Subrosa, but suddenly the stillness of the night was shot by the bang of a door slamming shut. I jumped, and when I looked back, the ghostly sisters had vanished.

Rushing through the murky garden to the front porch of the house, I discovered Fritz, shirtless, his hair slicked with sweat, smoking a cigarette. We nodded wordlessly to one another as I passed inside. The remainder of the night I devoted to writing furiously.

In the morning, I attempted to explain my vision of the Subrosa sisters to Fritz. He was sitting with his arm around his sex doll, Willow, sipping his coffee and caressing her bare shoulder.

"Willow really is perfect," he said, suddenly interrupting my story, leaning over to kiss the doll on the forehead. "After the Revolution, everyone will have one."

"Are you even listening to me?" I demanded, setting down my coffee.

"Yes, yes, your dream. Nightmares are sure to follow when you eat too much toasted cheese late at night."

I insisted to him that I never toasted the Parmigiano, that it was entirely cold, and that anyway I had fed much of it to a raccoon, but Fritz waved these objections away. I soon gave up trying to convince him of anything, realizing it was a waste of my energies. The winter was coming much sooner than I feared, and I had much work to do.

GROTESQUE

I relish the slap of my wet fingers against the plastic shell which covers my keyboard. It is not quite like the elaborate sound effects of the typewriters of ages past, but I don't want it to be. It has its own romantic aura, which is alive and especially mine.

I do not own a print of David's *The Death of Marat*. Any time I want to gaze at it, I must find it on the internet, or pick up my copy of *Marat/Sade* by Peter Weiss, which has the painting as its cover. Then there's the wonderful, ethereal, Gothic album *Deathconsciousness* by a band called Have a Nice Life—David's painting is here as well. I don't own the album (I don't own physical copies of any music), but when I stream it online I stare at the cover, at the figure of Marat in his bathtub, his head wrapped in a towel, one arm draped out of the tub, the other hand clutching a note with his final written words, his eyes shut in death, a stab wound in his chest from the cowardly assassin Charlotte Corday. Marat's unknown skin disease, which confined him to a bathtub for hours every day, is rendered gracefully invisible in David's exquisite painting. Marat's skin is clear, angelic in his martyrdom, purified in death.

I don't know the details of Marat's circumstances and his method for writing while in the bathtub, but I can only assume that I have it easier. While he was working with ink and paper—easily blotted and destroyed by even a single drop of water—I have the advantage of a laptop computer, encased in a waterproof shell. This allows me to periodically submerge my entire body, hands and all, in the water before surfacing to continue typing away, even as I drip dirty water directly onto the machine. If I wanted to, I could probably devise a way to keep the entire laptop underwater and write fully immersed, but my tub isn't deep enough for that. Anyway, this is perfectly comfortable—a sturdy caddy mounted over the tub, which at this moment holds my computer, a bottle of aquavit and a glass, and a mason jar filled with live minnows.

Like Marat, I can leave this clawfoot tub whenever I wish, but if I'm at home it's the most comfortable place for me to relax, eat, work, even sleep. Next to the tub in this dingy bathroom with its warped and discolored tiles, which serves also as my office and bedroom, there is a set of hooks. Here there hangs a black neoprene wetsuit, which is what I wear when I leave the apartment to go for walks or go swimming in the river. I zipper into my wetsuit, slip on boots and gloves, then throw a sweater or jacket on over everything. I wear a black gasmask with tinted goggles, which I suppose lends me a threatening and possibly ridiculous appearance, but I've grown to like it.

I like the feeling of rubber, the way it hugs my scales—it's comforting. And it's comforting to know that every inch of me is covered, invisible, safe.

Before I met Sloan, my exclusive method for seeking out human contact was visiting fetish clubs and parties around the city. I did this for two reasons. Firstly, such places were perhaps the only social environments where no one would bat an eye at someone dressed head to foot in black rubber. Secondly, I believed that among the kind of people who frequented such events I may find individuals open-minded enough to be my friends, real friends to whom I could disclose my true self. Perhaps there were others like me, or at the very least, people who would not be horrified, but rather fascinated, by what I am. Perhaps somewhere out there, even if it took me years to find her, there might even be a woman so bored and desensitized, a woman who could no longer be satisfied by ordinary men, a woman who was searching for some thrilling and forbidden monstrosity even if she didn't yet know what it was, in short, a woman so perverse that she might be able to love me.

It was a desperate dream, but I didn't go about it in a desperate way. I had to be patient, restrained. Given my situation, this was the only possible way for me to behave.

As it turned out, I never met anyone this way who I could become close to, but I did make a casual connection which proved decisive in the long run. At one party, I met a woman dressed head-to-foot in latex, not unlike myself—she wanted to be beaten with a fiberglass cane. Afterward, we held each other, pressed our bodies together while I squeezed her hips and breasts. She locked her thighs around me, rubbed herself against me. It was the closest

I'd ever come to sex—but it was safe, secret, everything mediated and concealed by shadows, loud music, rubber.

This woman, as it came out in a later conversation as we sat together on a sofa, was the arts editor for a trendy magazine. When I told her about my writing, she offered to show one of my stories to her friend in the fiction department. Two years and a handful of publications later, following the selection of one of my stories for a semi-prestigious literary award, I met Sloan.

I rarely go to fetish parties anymore, except occasionally to see old friends. I'm too busy with writing. Most days I spend writing copy for websites: descriptions of products I've never used, columns about cities I've never visited, tips for the kind of sex I'm not even capable of having. I've dabbled in astrological horoscopes, smut, and advice for pet owners, but what I most enjoy is writing book reviews. There is little demand for the reviews of the kind of books I typically read, and when I can publish them I don't always get paid—but at least, unlike the other stuff I write during the day, I can publish them under my real name (and by "real name," I mean, my literary as opposed to commercial *nom de guerre*). I make a fair amount of money these days, more than I need. But there's something about it that brings me satisfaction, much more than the old days of wallowing in the tub for hours fiddling with bad poems, drinking, and watching pornography, and barely making rent each month. Anyway, I'm saving quite a bit. Maybe one day I'll figure out what to do with it.

During the afternoon, while Sloan is at work, I write for money. When she comes home, we make dinner. After dinner, and into the night, I work on my fiction, sometimes taking a break to go for a walk or a swim, or to watch a film with Sloan, or fuck.

Because of my unique dietary requirements, we don't often eat take out. Early on, I tried to persuade Sloan to eat whatever she wanted and leave me to fend for myself, but she strongly disliked this idea and insisted that we share our meals. I have trouble digesting starches, and dairy makes me sick. Anything too rich or sweet is also no good. Before I met Sloan I subsisted almost entirely on fish heads and other discarded or spoiled bits which I acquired very cheap from a Chinese fishmonger. I paid the superintendent's daughter to fetch the fish parts and deliver them to me in a white bucket twice weekly. I kept the fish in the refrigerator not because I cared very much about freshness but to avoid alarming the neighbors with the stench of rotting fish (a smell which I somewhat enjoyed). I never cooked, but ate everything raw.

I had never thought to be ashamed of my diet before, but when Sloan first suggested we have dinner together I panicked, knowing full well how disgusting my customary meals would appear to her, and at that time afraid that any ordinary food would make me ill. At Sloan's insistence there followed then several weeks of experimentation, until we found those dishes we could enjoy together—grilled meat, boiled eggs, oysters, pâté. No more fish heads, though now my craving for raw fish is sated by live minnows from a bait shop.

Sloan doesn't spend every night with me. I would never expect her to. She brought a mattress into the bedroom, which until then had only functioned as a library, and often she sleeps there, wrapped in blankets, a manner of sleeping which I find entirely untenable. She enjoys sleeping with me in the empty bathtub, but complains of a sore neck, and of nightmares—for the sake of her health she can only do it once a week, at most.

At first, as Sloan later confessed to me, she thought the elaborate precautions to protect my anonymity were either attention-seeking theatrics or proof that I was a famous (or possibly disgraced) writer developing a new pen name. We exchanged emails, and when she insisted on meeting in person I explained that she could come to my apartment but that I would not, under any circumstances, remove my mask.

She was interviewing me on behalf of the magazine which had awarded the prize for my story. I had on a turtleneck sweater, latex gloves, and the gasmask which covered my face and helped disguise the slightly inhuman contours of my head. When Sloan arrived, she smiled and shook my hand, acting as if there were nothing at all out of the ordinary about my costume. There was a sofa and a chair in my otherwise bare living room, and we sat across from each other while she asked questions. Even through the gasmask, I could smell her breath, her skin, her scalp. It is, most likely, an illusion, a form of erotic synesthesia which makes the scent of beautiful women so especially intoxicating; it can't possibly be that I can really smell beauty. And yet, I have always been able to.

She was nervous. Her large, brown eyes and wide lips constantly flashed with little flights of manic irony. She tried to make obvious her awareness of the banality and uselessness of the interview questions, which she herself had not written. I must have done alright, despite how terrified I was, because at the end of the interview she turned off her recording device and asked me, again, candidly, the question she had already put to me on tape. Before, when she'd asked about the mask, I replied with evasive generalities, but now she was asking again.

The piece she was putting together about me was just a short profile, not very serious. And anyway, she had no stake in it, that was clear. She was cute, and the prospect of some real conversation with her, however fleeting, was enough for me. So, for better or for worse, I told her the truth. Or, rather, I told her a lie which hinted at the truth which I could not possibly reveal, not yet. I told her I had a disease.

I've always thought that I somewhat resemble, physically, certain demonic figures from medieval art. I say only somewhat, because while I am covered in dark green scales, possessed with yellow eyes and rows of carnivore's teeth, the resemblance stops there—the monstrosity of the medieval figures typically surpasses mine in its surreality. These grotesque creatures frequently are gifted with a multiplicity of faces, their bodies comprised of a dozen foul grinning sets of mouths and eyes. The chest and groin, the shoulders, elbows, and knees, all are demonic jaws, the body devouring and vomiting its own limbs, the genitals a hungry evil mouth. Sometimes in their claws they wield metal forks and arcane torture implements. Sometimes they have horns, and occasionally fur instead of scales. Their bestial attributes and the nightmarish superfluity of mouths is meant to represent lust, greed, and gluttony, a consumptive and devouring drive which is simultaneously associated with animal *nature* and an *unnatural* excess, both "beneath" and "beyond" humanity, more bestial than beasts themselves.

They are allegorical, I am real—that's the difference. Though, despite the modern distaste for allegory, it remains inevitable that we perceive each other and the world allegorically. Everyone does it, even the most ruthlessly pessimistic and "realistic" writers, because it is an inescapable dimension of our consciousness. You are afraid of a venomous serpent—why? Because it represents destruction. If you were incapable of perceiving this, you would be an idiot, and you would not survive very long in this world. Realists would argue that not all significance or meaning is allegorical, that certainly we can find meaning in the world, but that allegory is a primitive and illegitimate form of meaning-making based on crude and fanciful correspondences, analogous to the medieval practice of articulating magical linkages between astrology, minerals, plants, animals, spiritual concepts, etc., all of it a vast systematic hallucination.

We may reject this kind of allegory, but we cannot escape allegorical thinking in general. We must represent something. We cannot just be cold matter devoid of meaning, just amalgamations of culture and chemistry held together in the fragile web of the human form—yes, we are that. But we are also symbols, all of us. We represent something to each other. Not something simple, perhaps something exceedingly complex, so complex we cannot articulate it except through poetry or painting or by writing a novel or an endless series of novels. So yes, I know I represent something to Sloan, but I don't believe this obscures or erases my "human" complexity, my individual character and psychology with which modern writers are so obsessed. No, it is possible to have both, it is possible to have everything. In fact, it is necessary. Even when we believe we have unmasked the cliché to apprehend reality, we are merely substituting one layer of perception for another one, a deeper and more complex picture emerges and we discard what came before which now appears to us as an illusion. It's all illusion. The point is to create finer and more accurate and useful illusions. But even as we understand the viper more and more, it still must represent destruction.

It was only the next time we met that Sloan convinced me to remove my mask. We talked about music for a long time, about our shared love of Brian Eno and Dead Can Dance. We drank wine, which I sucked through a gasmask drinking tube. It was obvious to me why she was there. She knew that I knew, and it made us both nervous, because I already knew that she was too beautiful for me to resist doing whatever she told me to do, no matter the consequences.

Finally, she asked me about my disease. I told her it wasn't a disease, but a deformity. What kind? No, not a deformity at all, that wasn't right. I was just different. Different? Very, very different. Born like this, or possibly created. I didn't know who my parents were. I was born from the sewer, the river, the sea, probably I'd been dumped into the water as a baby. Or, possibly, spawned by some forgotten, despised race; perhaps I was the last, perhaps they were driven to such extremes of deprivation that they no longer remembered or cared how to raise their young. Or, conversely, I was not the last but the first, born from the toxic alchemy of polluted waters. There were endless possibilities, but none of them interested me much. The point was I survived. I lived in the shadows instinctively, hunted, learned. I watched humans and mimicked them. I watched snakes and fish and animals and mimicked them too. Slowly, I built this semi-civilized life.

Sloan didn't understand. I told her that I didn't either, and that anyway, it was impossible to explain. She just had to see. She promised not to be afraid.

The nervous tics, the little cringes of self-deprecating irony, which I found so cute and disarming, all of it had vanished during the course of this conversation. Her lips, trembling, parted, she smeared them fearfully with her tongue. I removed my mask.

She stared at me in silence. I gave her time, a lot of time. She looked away, then looked back at me, wringing her hands in her lap. When she spoke, despite how utterly strange her words should have been to me, somehow I was not surprised at all, because I could feel it, I could smell that she wanted it.

Are you going to kiss me?

Her eyes, narrowing and losing focus, seemed to surrender, as if she were sinking into a dream, a prophecy of what our love would mean. When I kissed her, she broke away and gagged, then quickly apologized and begged me not to stop. I kissed her again, felt her chest heave, and her whole body began to shake. I seized her arms, pressed her close to me. She wanted to be possessed, and so I possessed her, used her. It was sex, just sex, but for us it was something much worse. We both knew it without words, that like a pair of murderers we had shared in a crime that would bond us together forever.

After the award, publication was a bit easier. I sold more stories to magazines and journals. Sloan, acting as my unofficial agent, put me in touch with an editor, and a collection of my short stories was published. The critics tended to interpret my obsession with the inhuman as a metaphor for alienation, drawing lazy comparisons to Kafka, but reproving me for certain excessively "morbid" and "grotesque" tendencies. As I explained to Sloan in my first interview, and then to other journalists subsequently, it was never my intention to be purposefully macabre or even surreal. I was simply depicting, in fictionalized form, my experience of life and the world. No one, of course, took these remarks seriously, nor could anyone aside from Sloan ever guess how utterly frank and unmysterious I was actually being.

When Sloan comes home from work, I hear her keys jangling as she turns them in the lock, the door swings open, the cat meows (Sloan's cat, Marquis, who moved in along with her). We call to each other. She puts her things down, pours herself a glass of water, maybe makes herself a snack.

She strips off her clothes in the bedroom and pads into the bathroom naked. The bony ridge of her spine makes me think of pterodactyls and sauropods. The dimples on her buttocks make them seem like two buttoned pillows. The soles of her feet are dirty and black. I close my computer and remove the bathtub caddy, placing it on the ground as as she slides into the tub. Her breasts kiss the surface of the water. Her legs intertwine with mine. I caress her knees. She tells me about her day at work. I tell her about my writing. She stands up, water oozes off of her in dirty rivulets. I lean forward, my head is level with her groin. I kiss the lips of her vulva, gingerly nursing her until she opens for me.

We fuck in the drained bathtub, on the floor, occasionally in bed. I've never once used a condom. There's no chance that Sloan could ever become pregnant from me, as far as we know, though that doesn't stop her from talking about it. She shivers as I caress her with a webbed hand, leaving a trail of dirty slime along her skin. Her lips tremble the way they did when we first kissed. Her body contracts and draws close to mine, and she whispers:

Put a monster inside of me.

As I lay in my bathtub, I fold my hands together over my chest and observe Sloan as she brushes her hair in front of the mirror. I have never asked her to do so, but she knows I am obsessed with her hair, and so she always brushes it before me like this, completely nude. For our first Christmas together, I bought her an antique ivory hairbrush. When she uses it, wearing nothing else, standing in the yellow light of the bathroom, she looks like a ghost, or an angel.

I can smell when she's been with another man. I don't mean her cunt, I mean the pores of her skin. She exudes it, and my tongue tastes it on the air before she's even finished undressing. It disgusts me, but I don't resent her for it. I don't see it as a breach of faith. In fact, the opposite is the case. I am her disloyalty—not just to her other men, but to her entire race, her civilization. I am her secret. I am her depravity, her bestiality, her shame.

I often imagine what it would have been like to have been born in another time. Perhaps some would have worshiped me. More likely, I would have been killed. The modern world is worse, I think, because only now would they pity me. They would regard my entire existence as a disease to be mourned and, eventually, cured.

I however neither pity them in turn, nor resent them. I simply perceive them as animals, just like myself.

My stories are not my revenge against the world. Nor are they my attempt to reform or cure humanity, a race to which I have never belonged. No, I write for the simple and absurd reason that I don't know what else to do with my time. It's not as if I can go for walks in the park, take in the sun and the sight of innocent birds, take pleasure in the company of fine people, enjoy sports, restaurants, parties, all the things ordinary men and women do with their time. All of this is closed off to me. I am alone with words and art. And I'm content with that.

I don't feel shame. Most days I don't feel anything at all. But I am the world's shame. And so I will avoid the sun, and stick to the yellow lamplight of this bathroom.

I am done with writing short stories. I'm working on a novel now. A novel about a world of lakes and liquid bogs, a world of polluted rivers and dirty canals where every city is a sunken Venice, a world populated by men with webbed hands and the gills of fish, freaks with the slitted nostrils and forked tongues of serpents, ghouls with slime-covered frog-like skin, vampires with razor-sharp teeth and yellow eyes and scales. And above them, in the windows of inaccessible towers, beautiful women brush their shining hair.

I can see the reviews already…Gothic, surreal, morbid.

Grotesque.

THE PISS QUEEN OF GHOSTHEART MOOR

Would she cure his disease, or would she only make it worse?

It was impossible to know, because no one had ever seen her before, much less tasted her piss.

The glass of the train window was cold against Ambrose's forehead as he drifted in and out of dreamless sleep. The train ride was 11 hours, not including the frequent, unexplained stops at random intervals, in which the conductors exited the train and stalked up and down the tracks with their flashlights, inspecting the undercarriage. What did they think was there? An agonizing metallic peal, like a fantastic sword scraping tortuously across the flank of an iron monster, exploded from the depths of the train without warning each time one of these unscheduled stops was executed, and Ambrose would be yanked violently back from the precipice of sleep, the black poolside where he levitated in a semi-conscious trance of dilated time.

The train ride was 11 hours, but it must have ended up 13 with all those extra stops. At least Ambrose got to sit alone—his car was only half full, and each time the train made one of its regular stops more and more passengers shuffled off, and fewer and fewer got on. Ambrose feared the pale, plastic-wrapped sandwiches for sale in the dining car, and did not eat anything on the entire trip. He just slept, and drank water, and thought about piss.

What would a ghost's urine taste like? Ambrose had never even tasted ordinary human piss, but he could imagine it—pungent, acidic, an aftertaste of salt? Would a ghost's piss be the same? Or would it taste worse, like the putrid stench of old urine left fermenting on the sidewalk beneath construction scaffolding, or on the unwashed slats of a filthy outhouse. Or would it taste better, like dew, like meadows, like rainclouds or possibly even an angel's tears? Would it taste like white vinegar, or like champagne? Would it taste like iron, like raindrops slithering down a rusted metal railing? Would it taste like human skin and sweat, pheromones and pussy and whimpers of delight? Perhaps it would taste like his mother's milk, or like the milk of a goat or a horse. Perhaps it would taste like starlight, like an erotic minor chord struck with graceful fury on a portable harmonium, like poetry, like dreams, like memories, like an idea.

It wasn't just her piss, of course. He thought about her cold, fleshy thigh, how he would cool his flushed face against it. He prayed to the image of her bare calves, and of her naked feet, which might be washed and ruddy, or smudged gray with the dirt of the moor and the dust and ashes of her ruined castle. Would she allow him to sleep with his head nestled into her hips like a child? Would she caress him, her frigid corpse-like fingers stroking his weary neck, his shoulders, his cheek damp with tears? Would she kiss him? Would she drink her own piss, too? Would they drink it together in a marital sacrament? Would she, could she be his equal? Would they bathe in it, baptize themselves in her piss together? Would they become sorcerers? Would they become gods?

Milk-white vapor shrouded the landscape. Whenever the train stopped, or whenever Ambrose happened to open his eyes, he couldn't tell where he was or what time of day it might be. He thought about asking one of the conductors how far it was until the last stop, the appropriately named Creep's End, which was Ambrose's destination, but the conductors, with their black vests and jackets with silver buttons, their visored caps, and their large magic keys which opened every door on the train, exuded an intimidating, authoritarian brusqueness as they prowled up and down the cars on secret errands. Ambrose didn't ask them anything.

Was there a restaurant in Creep's End? Neither Joris nor Michael had mentioned anything about food. But Ambrose was starving. He was on the verge of surrendering to fate and going in for a gray tuna salad sandwich in the dining car when there came a final ear-splitting brake, and the conductor announced on the intercom: "Final stop. Creep's End."

Filing off the train with his backpack, his limbs stiff and bloodless, Ambrose stepped down into the chilly fog of the train station with the few remaining passengers. The mist had cleared half-way, almost as if the world were lifting up the edge of the blanket it was hiding under to peer nervously at Ambrose. Creep's End was like that, a bloodshot eye peeking out from beneath the fog. And indeed, there it was, red neon blazing through the mist like a sick electronic eye: the sign for a 24 hour diner.

Ambrose did not intend on delaying his journey. He wanted to set out into Ghostheart Moor as quickly as possible. But first, he needed to eat something, preferably a hamburger with French fries, accompanied by a cup of hot black coffee. This diner was quite possibly the ideal spot for such viands. Moreover, it was conveniently located only a short block from the train station. Ambrose smiled. He was very hungry, and the apparition of this neon sign, peeking so coquettishly from beneath the veil of mist, felt like a blessing on his entire desperate enterprise.

"I'd like a hamburger with French fries, and a cup of hot black coffee," said Ambrose to the waitress after examining the menu for several minutes to verify that these items were indeed on offer.

He was sitting in a booth by the window. The vinyl cushions of his seat, the lamination of the table and the plastic lamination of the menu, the plastic shades on the light fixtures, the glaze on the ceramic coffee mug—it felt like everything was coated in layers of some petrochemical shield which separated their raw materiality from contact with his skin. It was comforting.

The coffee was fine, the hamburger and French fries were good. It was everything that Ambrose wanted. He would be successful where Joris and Michael had failed, and this was why. The third time was the charm—isn't that what everyone said?

Joris hadn't been looking for the Piss Queen. At least, he didn't think that's what he was doing. In his head, he was just hiking. The German word is *wandern*, cognate with the English "wander." Today, most hiking is the exact opposite of wandering. It involves following a trail with the utmost obedience and orthodoxy because, we are warned, to do otherwise would be to risk ecological defilement of the land, and perhaps even bodily harm and death. Wandering, real wandering, is typically forbidden— except in certain regions, decolonized by entropy, where the roads and laws of man's kingdoms have fallen into ruin. Ghostheart Moor was one such place.

Joris was hiking, really hiking, that is to say, *wandering* in Ghostheart Moor, when he came upon the crumbling walls of an ancient castle. He wanted to get close to it, maybe to take some photographs of the exterior or even try to get inside, but he was stopped by a crazy woman dressed all in black. She chastised him, accused him of trying to drink the urine of the castle's mistress, and threatened to shoot him with a crossbow if he came any closer. Bewildered and terrified, Joris did not argue with the woman, whose crossbow was fully real, loaded with a heavy quarrel, and pointed at his head. He hiked back to Creep's End, got a room in the hotel, and took the train back to the city in the morning.

When Joris told his best friends Michael and Ambrose about his bizarre encounter, Michael became excited.

"You found the castle of the Piss Queen," explained Michael reverently. "Haven't you heard the legends? She is a ghost, a fairy, a nymph from the ancient world. It is said that her urine cures heartbreak. It's said that for some men with broken hearts, men who were born with broken hearts which nothing in the world can heal, her piss is the only cure. But her castle is protected by the Stalking Widow, a huntress who will kill any man who comes near. You're lucky you escaped with your life."

Ambrose speared the last French fry with his fork and used it to mop up the remnants of ketchup on his oval plate. The waitress, a sweet woman wearing a stained white apron, came by to refill his coffee cup and take away the empty plate.

"Are you going up onto the moor?" she said, her voice baroque with a sylvan country accent. She nodded toward Ambrose's backpack, which sat on the bench across from him in the booth.

"Yes," said Ambrose, wiping his mouth with his napkin. "Yes, I am. Any advice?"

She pursed her lips thoughtfully, leaning onto one side and pushing out her hip. "I don't think so," she said. "Just make sure you bring enough water."

Water? What would Ambrose need with water? He was after much more precious libations, which would quite possibly render water permanently redundant. He could not, of course, reveal the true nature of his expedition—to find the Piss Queen, to imbibe her fabled pee, perhaps even to dwell with her for all eternity in a hidden world of shadows and dreams. Ordinary people like the waitress must remain innocent of such things. It's not that Ambrose feared they would disbelieve him and denounce him as a lunatic—the real danger lay in the opposite direction. If they suspected, really suspected, that such things might be real, it would at best frighten and disturb them, and at worst, haunt them, obsess them, lure them toward mysteries which might spell insanity and destruction. Yes, for the masses of people it was indeed best that they should remain on the well-beaten trails marked out by collective wisdom.

Even someone like Michael, who in his own words had been preparing, consciously or unconsciously, his entire life for the "opportunity" (as he called it) of seeking out the Piss Queen, nearly lost his life from chasing ghosts (or perhaps, in the end, being chased *by* them). The doctors determined that his face had not in fact been grazed by a crossbow, as Michael insisted, but rather slashed by a piece of rusted barbed wire, probably while he was attempting to trespass into a sheep-fold. The resultant tetanus infection precipitated a near-fatal fever, accompanied by vivid hallucinations, which were later blamed for Michael's fantastic story about the woman in black metal armor, riding a reindeer, who shot a quarrel from her crossbow right past his head, lacerating his cheek and mangling his ear, and then said to him, while he stumbled backwards, screaming blindly with blood streaming down his neck and onto his expensive quilted nylon parka: "The next one goes into your brain."

Michael's fever-induced nightmares only came when the tetanus set in several days after he'd already made it back to the city. He'd already had time to tell the whole story to Joris and Ambrose well before the period of his alleged hallucinations, so it made little sense to dismiss his encounter with his assailant as nothing but the fantasy of a diseased brain. In the grips of the infection, wracked by paralysis and muscle spasms, Michael could not open his mouth and could barely breathe. Because Michael couldn't speak, the doctors asked Ambrose what had caused the injury. He told them the truth, but it wasn't to their liking, so they concocted their own false, hallucinatory version of events, involving the alleged barbed wire fence. Never mind that there were no sheep-folds in Ghostheart Moor—the pathways of modern thought, which guide men to familiar and safe conclusions, must not be strayed from.

Unlike Michael, Ambrose was up to date on his tetanus vaccination. Perhaps more importantly, he had a plan to deal with the woman in black, who legend named the Stalking Widow. He placed a hand on the pocket of his jacket, felt the secret thing that was there, safe and ready. And then he smiled knowingly at the waitress, who was still hovering there with the plate in one hand and the coffee pot in the other.

"Thank you," he said. "I'll be fine out there, don't worry about me. I'm ready for my check now, please."

It was late spring, and at those latitudes this meant that the sun would not set until quite late in the evening. The day was still milk-white, brimming with glowing mist, and would remain so for several more hours, long enough for Ambrose to reach the castle of the Piss Queen according to the map provided by Joris and confirmed by Michael's aborted expedition.

Ambrose finished his second cup of coffee, paid his bill with cash, gathered up his backpack, used the toilet, and then set out into the fog.

At the edge of town was a trailhead with a wooden kiosk featuring a map and some text about the geography of Ghostheart Moor, along with rules for walkers and backpackers (don't litter, try not to pitch your tent on top of certain rare species of lichen, etc.). There was no mention of the Piss Queen or her castle on these informational placards. As Ambrose set out along the dirt path, which would carry him away from Creep's End and into the heart of the moor before he would veer off into unmarked terrain to seek out the castle, he pondered this fact.

Why did no one else speak of the Piss Queen? Why was there no mention of her on the internet, or in any book? Compendiums of folklore and legend passed over her in total silence. The Piss Queen, her castle, her piss, and her faithful guardian the Stalking Widow—it was as if no one in the world had heard of them. Ambrose, in his researches prior to this expedition, not only found no mention of the Piss Queen and her attendant legends— there were also no legends, myths, or ghost stories of any kind associated with Ghostheart Moor whatsoever. Whatever romance or nightmare lent its lurid name to that land had long been forgotten, or possibly erased from memory by censorious colonizers. The place now was a spiritual and historical, as well as ecological and economic, wasteland, giving life to nothing but the heather, bracken, lichens, and a few scattered species of rodent and bird.

Perhaps the legend of the Piss Queen was not Medieval, then, but purely modern. And, moreover, so rare, so obscure as to be confined strictly to a sub-sub-culture consisting of three individuals—Joris, Michael, and Ambrose. After Michael recovered from tetanus, and after Ambrose's researches into the Piss Queen had proven utterly barren, he pressed Michael to explain how he had come to learn the details of the legend. Evasive, tortured, finally Michael confessed that he didn't know. The legend was simply something he had always known, even if he had never articulated it, even if he had never named it until Joris told the story of his encounter, at which time the details rushed into Michael's mind and out of his lips, and he found himself blurting out the full-fledged lore which until then had been only a formless and shifting spectral fantasy brooding in the wounded recesses of his heart.

Indeed, had not Ambrose also felt a chill of recognition when Joris first recounted his experience of the castle and the Stalking Widow, and an even more profound sense of nostalgia and fascination when Michael explained the legend? It had all made sense, deeply and immediately.

Why hadn't anyone else heard of the Piss Queen? Why hadn't anyone else discovered the castle? It was almost as if it had been made for them exclusively, like it was waiting for them. Despite its ruinous appearance, the castle according to Ambrose's research had no historical reality. It was entirely phantasmagorical, non-existent, a mirage conjured from pure desire. Private, secret, impossible—and yet, the stitches on Michael's face and ear were testament to the brutal, undeniable force of its very real existence.

Ambrose paused to catch his breath at the top of a hill. There it was—an ancient, solitary tree, blasted in twain by a bolt of lightning. Its blackened trunk was covered with innumerable carved initials, names, declarations of love, promises of eternity, hearts pierced with arrows. From the base of the tree, to the midpoint of its trunk where it split apart into two dead halves, and up to the unreachable branches there flourished these savage markings. This was the unmistakable landmark which meant, according to Joris's instructions, it was time to leave the trail and march off into the reddish bracken.

Ambrose stood before the tree, and peered between its broken halves. The fog was dense, but he could see the upward slope of another broad hillside, tangled with bracken and scattered with gray boulders. If he climbed through the tree and walked straight onwards, he would find his way.

The trunk, carbonized by fire and then polished by one or two hundred years of youthful lovers' hands and knives, was smooth. Climbing through it was the most natural thing in the world, the wood welcomed Ambrose's hands and the gap between the halves accommodated his body perfectly. He experienced another surge of confidence like what he'd felt in the diner. Others had failed, but he would succeed. This was his story. It was all laid out for him. No one else could find the Piss Queen because she was meant for no one else. The third time was the charm. Ambrose climbed through the tree and left the trail.

The rich burgundy of the tangled bracken appealed to Ambrose. It recalled the pubic hair of certain fair-skinned lovers of his past, friends and acquaintances he had made love with, but not loved, not truly. He wished to pause and touch it, smell it, but he did not want to stray from his course. It was hard enough to walk in a straight line already. In such dense fog, if he stopped to appreciate the flora he was likely to become disoriented.

Having made it down the hill, he began to climb the next one, which was less steep but taller. Past it was another hill, and then a third one. At the far side of this third hill was a ravine. Dead, stunted trees huddled along the banks of a dry creekbed. Descending carefully, Ambrose reached the creekbed, turned left, and began to walk. Unless he'd made some mistake, this creekbed would lead him eventually to the ruins of the Piss Queen's castle.

The truth was, Ambrose had known from the start that both Joris and Michael's heartbreak was not worthy of the Piss Queen. When Michael had insisted on setting out in search of her, Ambrose remained silent, knowing in some secret way that Michael would fail and his turn would come. Now here he was, his instincts justified so far. In the pocket of his jacket he held the key to his triumph, and in his heart he guarded a pain supreme, nurtured from infancy. The cold, damp moor gnawed Ambrose's ears with its ghastly toothless gums, but his heart was warm. For the first time in years he had found hope again, long after he had consigned it to the tear-soaked pillows of childhood. Now it was reborn, a sponge dripping warm with blood, a reopened wound, rearing from dormancy to breathe and bleed desire into every inch of body and mind.

It was hard to say how long Ambrose had been followed. The mist was so thick, and his stalker was so quiet, that she could very well have been behind him since the moment he set out onto the moor. It was only when the ravine opened out onto a plain filled with stunted trees, and the clouds lifted to unveil the dark gray, antique masonry looming on the distant hill, that Ambrose realized, with his destination within sight, its guardian must be nearby. It was then that he looked behind himself and perceived the dark silhouette of a mounted figure in the mist.

According to the accounts of both Joris and Michael, she would not attack him without warning. She would confront him first, at which point he would have his opportunity. And so, not allowing himself to be intimidated, he proceeded through the thicket of brown ferns and dead trees, reaching the base of the hill which wore like a crown upon its summit the fabled fortress.

The mist cleared more and more, but the air became ever colder as Ambrose neared his target. Glancing occasionally over his shoulder, he watched his hunter grow closer and more distinct. He began to perceive the contours of her armor, black and cruel with spikes and flourishes. He saw that, just as Michael had reported, her steed was no pony but a handsome reindeer with a rack of huge velvet antlers. Soon the beast was close enough that Ambrose could hear its footsteps on the turf and the snuffle of its snorting nostrils blasting plumes of white fog into the air.

At the summit of the small hill the castle waited in silence. At the center of the maze of crumbled walls and old foundations, the ancient keep stood strong, its narrow slitted windows filled with darkness, but the state of its wooden door, old but somehow preserved, promised life.

"I knew you would come," came a voice from behind Ambrose. "Your stupid friends came first, but I knew that you would follow, even after what I did to the last one."

Ambrose turned to face the Stalking Widow. Her crossbow, crafted from the same dark phantom stuff as her armor, was loaded, but she held it facing the earth. Her face was masked by a grotesque helmet which lent her the visage of a grimacing phantom.

"I'm not like them," said Ambrose. "They didn't deserve to see your Queen. But I'm different. And I can prove it."

The Stalking Widow scoffed, and her reindeer snorted and shuffled its hooves, as if sharing her disbelief. "*My* Queen?" she said. "You think that she is *my* Queen?"

Ambrose hesitated. "Is that not why you guard the castle?" he said.

"I do not guard the castle," said the Stalking Widow, her voice filled with bitterness. Her words ached with deep suffering, but at the same time it was like she took sadistic pleasure in revealing the truth. "I couldn't care less about this wretched castle. In fact, I despise it. No. I'm here because I want *revenge*."

"Revenge?" Ambrose whispered in bafflement, the word barely escaping his lips in a puff of frozen breath.

"That's right," she said tauntingly. "Revenge against whoever comes here. Your friends, yes. But especially *you*."

"No," said Ambrose. "No. I'm different. I'm not like them. Look."

He withdrew it from his pocket, then, his magic key. It was a small, translucent plastic shell with a green plastic lid. Such shells, which were containers for random toys and baubles, were dispensed from vending machines in supermarkets and shopping malls for 25 or 50 cents. The first and only time Ambrose had placed a coin into one of these machines, which he did on a whim as a child, this very container with the green lid tumbled out of the machine. Inside it was a black plastic ring. In that moment,

Ambrose knew that this ring was meant for his true love, and he kept it safe ever since that day. For, while Ambrose had gazed upon true love, it had never gazed back. There had never been one who might receive his childish gift. He gave up, but he never forgot, and his gift remained—inviolate, pure, not defiled but blessed with his silent suffering. Even as Ambrose tortured himself, clawing his skin and heart with nails of anger, his gift remained perfectly clean, whole, encased in plastic, waiting for this day.

Ambrose showed the ring to the Stalking Widow. "This is my gift for her," he said. "My pain, my love, is real."

Climbing down from her reindeer, the Stalking Widow stepped towards Ambrose, her heavy boots crushing the ferns in her path.

"How dare you show this to me," she hissed as she stood near him, close enough to perceive what lay in his open palm. "How dare you."

Her breathing was heavy. She was trembling. Her eyes glared fiercely out at him from the slit in her helmet's visor.

Afraid that she might knock the ring from his hand, Ambrose withdrew it close to his chest. Her manner disturbed him. He could not understand her behavior or speech. All he could think to say was: "Who are you?"

The Stalking Widow lifted the helmet off of her head and threw it onto the earth, unveiling her ruddy, tear-stained face, her nose dripping with snot, her blonde hair lank with sweat.

"Well, then?" she said. Her voice was still full of irony and bitterness, but beneath it was a glimmer of hope. "Do you recognize me?"

Ambrose studied her face, her sorrowful eyes, the strands of yellow hair plastered to her forehead. She bit her pink lip to stop it from trembling. Her face was faintly familiar, as if he had seen it somewhere long ago in a dream or a film, but he could not remember where.

"I'm sorry," he said at last. "I don't remember."

"Well," she replied. "I remember you. You see...I loved you once."

A spasm of pain escaped her lips like a hiccup, but she breathed deeply through her nose and blinked away the tears. Removing a white kerchief from around her neck, she mopped her face and wiped her nose.

"When we were young," she went on, her voice flattened by her congested nose. "Oh, when we were young...I knew all three of you. Joris, Michael, and you. None of you gave me the time of day. We spoke on occasion, but I'm not surprised you don't remember me. I tried to get your attention, oh yes, I tried. I changed the way I dressed to better suit your tastes. I listened to the right music, read the right books, learned the right politics. None of it mattered. I remained like a phantom to you, even though I was real, *so real*, so warm and ready and waiting for you. My *love* was real."

"If you waited for me," said Ambrose, "then why are you called Widow? Who was your husband?"

"You were my husband, in my dreams!" she cried. "But now those dreams are dead."

She wept openly now, unable or unwilling to stem the flow of tears and mucus.

"Do you think I like living like this?" she said. "I hate it. I hate this bitterness. I hate the hatred that I feel for you. But you're to blame for all of it! How can you be so blind? You're in love with a ghost. I'm right in front of you, alive and warm and full of love, but you prefer the cold skin of a corpse. You're going to throw your life away, for what? A ghost, an illusion! Why? So you can drink her piss? You think that's going to make you feel something? You think that's going to make you feel loved? You'd rather drink her piss than kiss me, is that it? You'd rather be poisoned and degraded by her, you'd rather be her slave, than be my prince. Is that right? Answer me, goddamnit!"

"Yes," replied Ambrose, his eyes cast down in shame, but his spirit lucid and his voice resolute.

The Stalking Widow cried out then, a sustained shriek of agony and grief, as she lifted her crossbow haphazardly and fired it directly into Ambrose's leg.

In the first moment the pain was sharp and extreme, and caused Ambrose to immediately break out in a cold sweat of panic. He couldn't breathe. And then a raging flood of excruciating heat burst from his thigh. It was almost as if the blood pouring from the wound was acid seeping into his flesh and scorching his nerves with pain. Crumpling onto the turf, he gasped for breath, then howled in anguish. The plastic ring, in its plastic shell, slipped from his fingers and fell to the ground.

His assailant's scream had collapsed into weeping. "How could you do this to me?" she said through a veil of tears and snot. "How could you do this to me?"

Shambling away, she climbed back onto her reindeer. The animal snorted and groaned. She called out "*Hiya!*" and Ambrose could hear, and feel, the reindeer's galloping hoofbeats in the earth as it took her away.

Ambrose was dizzy with pain and fear, but he had regained his breath. He looked at his leg. The quarrel had penetrated his thigh completely, with one end sticking out from either side. Dark blood covered his pant leg and the grass and the ferns. It was pouring out of him—too much of it. He realized that his femoral artery may have been severed and that he might bleed to death.

On the grass nearby, next to the black helmet which the Stalking Widow had abandoned on the ground, there lay her rumpled kerchief. Apparently she had dropped it, either on accident or intentionally, as a memento of her grief. It was cold and wet with her tears and snot, but when Ambrose grabbed it he found that it was large enough for his purposes. He wrapped the kerchief around his upper thigh, above the wound, and tied it as tight as he possibly could. The wetness of tears and blood lent an elasticity to the fabric which made it easier to pull tight.

His hand slick with blood, he grasped the plastic ring case from where it had fallen in the grass, and held onto it.

Afraid that attempting to stand would only aggravate his wound, Ambrose began to drag himself toward the castle door. Positioning himself on his side, so that his bad leg would not touch the earth, he pulled himself toward the doorway, leaving a trail of blood in the grass and ferns behind him.

Would she cure him, would she save his life, or would she only make it worse? Ambrose didn't know what to believe, but if he could reach her, if he could just taste the grail of her love, he would know solace at least for one moment of his life.

Ambrose was thirsty. He was close to the door now, it loomed above him, but his arms grew weak. He needed water, her water—the water which had washed through her body, cleansed her blood and her skin and her organs, absorbed her toxicity, her pollution.

To drink her piss was to betray nature and to assert the supremacy of desire. It was bestial and divine at once, this corruption of life. And that which was real had to be sacrificed for this, this mystery, this unreal dream, this lie.

THE REAL SIMON DICK

I had just returned from a gorgeous Saturday afternoon at the shooting range with my housemate Francis when, upon going downstairs to enjoy a can of beer on the sofa, I discovered Simon Dick was living in my basement. For those of you who don't know, Dick was, at that time, the most prominent white nationalist in the country, although he refused the label of white nationalist, neo-Nazi, etc., preferring to outfit his backward ideology in more fashionable dress. He was simply a *neo-traditionalist*, someone deeply concerned with his European *cultural heritage*; he liked to describe his positions as "alternative" and "radical." This intellectual cowardice made his ideas all the more repugnant. "What we call for," he famously proclaimed, "is *peaceful* ethnic cleansing." It's your brain that needs cleansing, Simon—but don't worry, we'll do it *peacefully*.

How strange then, and unexpected, actually alarming, to discover this man sitting on the sofa in the basement of our house, smoking cannabis, *my cannabis*, out of our green plastic bong. As my housemates and I were well-known and active radicals, my first thought was that Dick's presence was malevolent. Were his ugly thugs hiding in the closet and the bathroom, waiting to spring out and attack me when he gave the signal? But no, it couldn't be, because Simon was stupid with drugs and beer, his eyes glazed over and red, his body melted into the sofa. This was not the slick bourgeois villain I had seen in so many clips of interviews and speeches, but a slouching, degenerate pizza fiend, a nuked-out wastoid…And yet it was unmistakably him—the stylish undercut (the hair buzzed on the sides, longish but neatly combed on top), cleft chin and baby face, blue eyes, diminutive stature, even the thin black tie and khaki blazer. Everything was there except for his signature smirk, that arrogant sneer which he always wore except when he was bellowing, red-faced, about immigrants, feminism, and the Marxist conspiracy to undermine the West. But here he was neither sneering nor frenzied. His face and shoulders were slack with a disarming, drugged, melancholic innocence.

He was not here to do us any harm, that much was clear. But what about his own safety? Wasn't he afraid? Maybe he didn't know who we were when he arrived (whenever that was), but hanging on the wall right behind the sofa where he was sitting was a 5 by 3 foot anarcho-syndicalist flag—the black and the red! Anti-fascist and left-wing punk stickers were all over the mini-fridge, and if he'd taken a leak he surely would have noticed the portrait of Lenin hanging over the toilet. This was clearly a punk house, a hard left, that is to say *real*, punk house, inhabited by the kind of people who routinely shut down Simon Dick's rallies with stink bombs, pepper spray, and road blockades, the kind of people who weren't afraid to smash windows, to use bricks and baseball bats and Molotov cocktails to defend and escalate the struggle of the workers when they took to the streets. The kind of people who might pose a real threat to Simon Dick's personal well-being.

I say the kind of people, and perhaps we were that kind, though we as particular individuals, those of us who lived in that house, we were not like certain young radicals, adventurists always eager for a fight. No, we took violence very seriously, and it wasn't something we engaged in frivolously. Violence to us was a specter haunting the future, something to be put off until absolutely necessary. That's why Francis and I had gone to the shooting range, why we went every other Saturday. Yes, it was relaxing and fun, but we wanted to be ready for whatever might happen. We lived in a time of crises upon crises, and we simply had to be prepared.

But nothing, really nothing could have prepared me for encountering Simon Dick stoned in my basement that Saturday, that *particular* Saturday…for you see, just that morning, before heading to the shooting range with Francis, I had been officially declared sane by the Center for Psychic Surveillance. In those days it was all too common for a radical such as myself to be flagged by the CPS, which never regarded as pathological the utterly suicidal insanity of empire and ecological ruination, but frequently labeled as insane those who challenged the rapacious nihilism of this hegemonic order. Granted, it was not just my political proclivities which had drawn the attention of the CPS. I had, it is true, experienced certain other symptoms, but these were usually only brought on by drugs. Anyway, it was supposed to be a pleasant Saturday, a day off, and in the evening I had plans to celebrate with my friends. What would happen now?

Standing at the bottom of the stairs, staring at Simon Dick as he ripped that bong, these thoughts raced through my head, but as he exhaled a massive plume of cannabis smoke, I realized I had to act. And so I said:

"Hey."

Simon turned to regard me through the dense cloud of white bong smoke, his red eyes glowing like coals.

"Hey," he said. "You gonna hit this?"

I won't recount the next hour in detail, except to say that it was among the most uncomfortable hours of recent memory. We smoked, cracked open some beers, watched a couple of funny videos on the internet, and all the while I circled around the question of how he got into our house, but all I got in reply were vague assurances. He was friends with Amelia, he had been at the party and had crashed last night, and now was waiting for a ride from James. Amelia? James? I didn't know these people. And I didn't know about any party the night before.

As we hung out I began to feel pity for the man. He seemed to have not the slightest idea of the situation he was in, so when the time came for me to betray him it would be completely unexpected. I couldn't help but feel guilty about the inevitable turn that things would take.

I left him on the couch while I took a shower. Stoned, my fingertips were made of Styrofoam and my scalp was sensitive, provocative with perplexing visions.

I found Francis hanging out with Marek in the kitchen. They were whispering about Simon.

"Hey," said Marek when I came in, wearing my bathrobe, to grab a piece of fruit. "Who's that guy downstairs?"

"I believe it's Simon Dick," I explained.

"See, I told you," said Francis.

"How is that possible?" demanded Marek.

"Let me get dressed first," I said. "Then I'll take care of it."

But I didn't take care of it. I didn't know how. After I got dressed, I went back to the basement to talk to Simon. His ride, James, was still nowhere to be found. It was getting dark, and I had plans to celebrate that night. One thing led to another, and I didn't quite know how to tell Simon to fuck off. Somehow he ended up on the train with us to the bar.

"What are we going to do?"

I was with Marek in an alley outside. We were smoking cigarettes and doing a couple bumps of crushed amphetamine.

"I don't know," I said, furiously rubbing my nose. "We'll ditch him here. Wait till he goes to take a piss then we'll all split."

Inside, they were selling flying drones at the bar for $1,000 apiece. And those suckers were buying them! There were television screens everywhere, playing sports and sitcoms with the frantic clown-like screams of the actors all silenced by the dance music blasting from the sound system. Drunk idiots piloted the drones, which hummed overhead and occasionally smashed into TV screens in showers of sparks. It was the worst bar I'd ever seen in my life. Who picked this place? I was on the verge of a panic attack while I cowered at the bar, waiting for the bartender to mix my whiskey sour. I was so wound up that I almost jumped out of my seat when David clapped me on the shoulder.

"Hey, man," he said. "Congratulations."

We shook hands. David had long, unkempt hair tucked loosely behind his ears, a thick mustache, and sideburns. He wore a bomber jacket, black jeans, Doc Martens, and a pair of aviator sunglasses hanging from the collar of his death metal t-shirt. From the way he dressed, and from his upright, aggressive posture and sharp gestures, it was easy to overlook the fact that his ectomorphic frame could probably be knocked over by a strong breeze.

Leaning on the counter, clutching his aluminum bottle of cheap lager, he nodded his head to a booth in the corner where Simon was sitting.

"Look," he said. "Do you see who that is?"

"I can't tell," I lied uneasily.

"That's *Simon Dick*," David bit his lower lip, his nostrils flaring, his eyes going wide with a sudden feral glee. "What should we do?"

"I don't know…"

"What the fuck is he doing here? Should we take him out back?"

"I don't think so."

"What is he doing here…"

"He's with me."

"*What?*" David glared at me with genuine bewilderment, which slowly dawned into fear.

"I can't explain right now. It's complicated."

Glancing left and right, he leaned forward. "Are you *undercover?* Are you fucking *infiltrating…*"

"I don't know. I mean, no. It's too much to explain right now."

David regarded me with grave apprehension. "I hope you know what you're doing," he remarked finally. "But I thought we were celebrating tonight…"

"Yes, I know. Don't worry about it. We're going to ditch him. And then let's forget the whole thing, alright? I want to get out of this place anyway."

Furiously sucking my bourbon, I glanced around the packed bar, at my friends, at the faces of strangers, at Simon Dick who was gazing disconsolately at the rings of condensation on his table like someone in the grip of terrible reflections.

"Damn him, won't he piss?" I hissed under my breath.

At that moment a drone crashed into one of the speakers. It fell from its perch on a shelf, swung down on a black cable, and smashed into the wall. The music abruptly stopped. The drone itself became lodged in an artificial fern, where its motorized propellers spun uselessly and emitted a painful grinding noise. A moment later it burst into flame.

"Let's get out of here, please," I said, grabbing Marek's arm as he walked near me to get a better view of the wreck. The whole bar was crowding around, jeering and exclaiming.

"What about Dick?" he whispered.

"Let's slip out now. He's distracted."

Oblivious to the commotion, Simon Dick was still lost in his drink. What was he dreaming about? I didn't want to know. I was already following Marek outside. David was with us. We signaled to Francis.

"Can we go somewhere cool, please?" I insisted.

"I'll take care of it," said David authoritatively. He had already hailed a cab and the four of us were climbing in, him in the front passenger seat.

"Club Nacht," he said to the driver. "You know the place?"

"Sure, sure."

But as Francis pulled shut the door, it stopped, as if stuck, caught on something. A terrible moon appeared, the face of Simon Dick, suddenly peering into the taxi.

"No, no, no, no, no," I cried. "We're full. No room. There's no room."

"Drive," said David calmly but decisively to the cabbie. "Just drive. Drive. Drive. Drive. Drive."

Francis's feeble grip on the door handle grew weaker and weaker, until finally his fingers collapsed and he withdrew his hand into his lap.

We cried out in protest, but could not resist, as Simon Dick climbed into the backseat of the cab, crawling onto our laps until he was lying face up on top of us. He clasped his hands over his stomach and shut his eyes as if he were about to be anesthetized for a surgical procedure.

"What are you doing?" protested the driver. He was an ethnic European with a sharp, angry accent. "You must have seatbelt. Seatbelt!"

In the confused yelling and accusations which followed, Simon remained perfectly still on our laps. Our words completely failed to dislodge him. David was furious at the cowardice of those of us in the backseat, but became silent when I pointed out that he too was unwilling to drag Simon out of the cab. Finally the cabbie gave up and pulled away from the curb, denouncing us angrily, promising to impose extra fees against us. He muttered vague threats as to what would happen if the police pulled us over, but thankfully this did not occur.

Nacht was a couple of miles away, in a hipper, more isolated and impoverished neighborhood. The tropical pinks and blues of the apartment clapboards were faded and peeling, half the windows boarded up or taped over, the gutters and sidewalks littered with trash, the brick walls fresh with dazzling graffiti. Everyone was completely silent for the duration of the drive. When we arrived, the cabbie insisted on being paid extra, and David took care of it as promised while Simon Dick wriggled off of our laps like a huge caterpillar.

The bar was on the corner. Above the door was a polished black globe the size of a large man curled in the fetal position. Beneath the globe, a sign in blinding neon white: COME ON IN.

Punks and bohemian types smoked cigarettes and stared at the glowing blue screens of their mobile phones on the sidewalk outside. I had never been to Nacht, but I'd heard of it, and it was obvious that among the trendy clientele there would be plenty of radicals. Practically every young anarchist and socialist knew Simon Dick, and I became suddenly terrified that he would be recognized. If it somehow came out that my friends and I were chumming with Dick, our reputation would be ruined.

Unless, of course, we could still manage to play it off as if we'd arranged the whole thing intentionally, as a prank, or something worse.

"Are you alright, man?"

It was Marek, speaking to Francis, who looked like he was on the verge of tears. We were still outside, hanging back while I smoked a cigarette. Simon Dick had already gone inside.

"What's going on?" I said.

"It's Simon, fucking Simon," said Francis through gritted teeth. He took a deep, ragged breath.

"What happened?" demanded David.

"When he was laying on our laps…His butt was right on my lap. And…I got hard, man. I fucking got hard." Francis, grimacing, covered his eyes with his hand, pressing his temples, then pinching the bridge of his nose as he fought back tears.

"That motherfucker," said David, his nostrils flaring. "I'm going to kill that motherfucker."

"Why don't we just leave," I suggested, blowing smoke out of the corner of my mouth. "He went inside. Fuck him. Someone will probably recognize him in there and do something about it. Let's get out of here, head somewhere chill…"

"No, no, fuck that," said David. "We're not letting that fucking goblin ruin your special night, man. We're supposed to be fucking *celebrating*. And what he did to Francis…"

David closed his eyes and shook his head, consumed with an unspeakable rage.

Marek was trying to comfort Francis. "Come on, man," he said, patting him on the shoulder. "It's not your fault. It's not your fault."

Francis sniffled and rubbed his eyes. "Do we have any coke?"

We stood behind a dumpster in an alley nearby and did some lines off the back of Marek's steel cigarette case. I felt like absolute hell. I considered playing sick, calling a cab for myself and going home, but I was afraid of what I might find there. I was increasingly, irrationally afraid that no matter where I ran, I would be confronted by the pathetic face of my enemy. The thought of his face filled me with disgust and pity, but I was powerless to do anything about it. I became convinced that it really was no mistake, that he was the real Simon Dick, that the clean-cut bully I'd seen in images was an act he put on, but now we had seen the real him. Lost, alone, impotent, and drugged—just like the rest of us.

The inside of the bar was just as dark as the street. The light and temperature were the same, to the point where I was unsure whether or not there was a roof on the building. Were we in a dark, expansive courtyard? I couldn't be certain. Fragrant flowers and ferns were stuck in recesses in the damp, brick walls, and were arranged across the bar in a way that made it difficult to wave down the bartender. Cold, thumping, gothic electronica painted everything with a darkly erotic ambience.

"Hey, how are you?"

It was Annie, the girl I was in love with, suddenly appearing from between the dark ferns. I had no idea she was bartending here. And now she was smiling at me, her tattooed arms spread out and gripping the lip of the bar, loose strands of her red hair, escaped from their ponytail, stuck on her damp forehead. I had been leaning forward, and now we were close and I could almost smell her skin.

"I need a beer."

"I got you."

Leaning my elbow on the bar, I peered out at the dimly lit club and realized we were on some kind of terrace looking out over a sunken courtyard that was crowded with trees and pyramidal structures lit with pink and green neon. We must have been elevated twenty feet or more above these secret gardens, which were connected to the terrace by a narrow brick stairway.

Annie set down a red plastic cup filled with draft beer, along with a shot of tequila and a wedge of lime.

"Tequila's on me," she said. "But you have to tell me what's wrong."

I took the shot, sucked the juice from the lime.

"I'm just worried about the future," I said. "What if things don't work out, you know? I mean, with the Revolution and everything. What if…"

I didn't know what else to say, but I didn't have to think of anything. I was saved by a sudden explosion— blue and green fireworks were being set off in the buried gardens. The gunshot blast was followed by the sound of fizzling sparks, and then whooping and cheers. The explosion itself was barely high enough to be visible from my vantage point—it had gone off around the height of the treetops and the pyramids. This hardly seemed like a sober trajectory for firing explosive rockets, even small ones.

"What's going on down there?" I asked Annie.

"It's an art installation," she explained, unperturbed by the fireworks. "They just installed it this morning."

"What is it?"

"There's a party in the courtyard around those pyramids. You go inside one to get away from everything. Once you're inside, you can go crazy…"

"What?"

"You can go crazy—I mean, you can do whatever you want. No one's watching," Annie smiled mischievously. "But you can still see the people outside, and the fireworks, so you know what you're missing. It's supposed to be very relaxing. Maybe you should try it—you look like you need it."

"Yes, maybe that's what I need," I admitted. "Just to get away from everything for a while."

Another blast and sparkle of fireworks, the momentary boom of light casting Annie's face and skin, my hands and my drink, all in blue. I picked up my beer.

"Thanks, Annie," I said.

"I'll see you around. And hey, I heard about your good news. Congratulations."

The brick floor of the bar area was slightly damp, as was the iron railing at the edge of the terrace, almost as if it had recently rained. Sidling through the crowded bar, I came to the railing and leaned over to look down at the sunken courtyard. The sharp, narrow pyramids, made of smooth gray metal with blinking strips of neon along their angles, were scattered amid the wet grass and trees. A murky expanse of trees lay beyond, stretching out into the shadows. Amid the pyramids, people danced and shouted and drank beer, and gathered in circles around where the fireworks were being launched.

I carefully descended the slippery steps, and was just admiring one of the pyramids all lit up with pink neon, surrounded by some punks in black cut-off denim shorts drinking beer and playing with a beach ball, when I heard the shouting.

"I need to know, Goddamnit! Who's inside that thing?"

I slithered through the wet grass, which dampened my shoes and pants, in the direction of the fight. It was David, fuming, one lanky arm stretched out to jab his finger at the installation. He was face to face with a woman wearing a long white dress covered with an expansive design of a Japanese-style octopus encircling her body. She had on a black beret, and her earrings were heavy black globes much like the unmarked sphere that hovered above the entrance to the club. Her arms were crossed and her long face was drawn down with consternation.

"I can't tell you who's in there," she replied angrily, "and I can't open the door."

A growing number of people had gathered around them to witness the scene. A professional photographer kneeled in the grass and snapped a picture of the altercation in a crackle and flash of bluish light.

"Simon Dick might be inside that pyramid," snarled David. "Do you have any idea who that is?"

"I don't care if Genghis Khan is inside. Someone is having an artistic experience. I'm not going to allow you to violate my creation. Fascist!"

Stunned, David's face opened and elongated into a mask of amazement. "Fascist? *I'm* the fascist?"

Pushing through the giggling crowd, I left David and the artist, who were still exchanging furious language. I went to the pyramid next door, which seemed to be available. A gallery assistant in a smart black dress smiled and opened the triangular door on the side of the structure.

"Stay in as long as you like," she said reassuringly. "Just press the red button if you need help."

I ducked through the portal and found myself at the base of the tall, three-sided pyramid. The attendant immediately shut the door behind me. Inside, there was nothing but a dubious cushioned bench, not unlike something you'd find in an airport or bus terminal. It smelled clean enough, so I sat down.

The walls of the pyramid, from the inside, were screens of dull bluish light, through which the human figures outside were silhouetted. I saw the gallery assistant, and farther back the crowd which had gathered around David and the artist as they yelled and pointed at one another. Behind me, I could see the punks still playing with the beachball. But their shapes were blurred, their movements stilted and fragmented like stop motion photography. Another round of fireworks went off—the sound was muffled, but I could see the shadow of sparks, and the pale cloud of smoke left hanging in the air.

Noticing a used condom on the floor, I drew my feet up onto the bench, hugging my knees to my chest. I sipped my plastic cup of beer and watched the silhouette of the beachball clipping through the air from one person to the next. I much preferred watching them to what was happening on the other side, where no doubt the bouncers had already been summoned and soon David would wind up with another broken nose, or worse.

Next to the door was a large red button. I did not think I would need to push it, but for a moment I allowed myself to imagine what if would feel like if I did. The gallery assistant would open the door, perhaps someone else would rush over as well, and they would peer in through the door which was very much like the miniature door of a child's playhouse, and they would say "Is everything alright?"

THE GIRL WHO SUCKED TEA FROM HER SWEATER

To protect her anonymity I'm not going to use her real name. I tried to think of a fake name, but nothing seemed to fit, so instead I'm just going to call her the girl who sucked tea from her sweater. In fact, this is how I referred to her inwardly in the weeks before I learned her name. Even after I knew who she was, I still thought of her that way. I preferred to. I still do prefer it. I still want to protect her anonymity, for her sake, but also for mine.

I'll get straight to the point. She was wearing a cotton sweater, three or possibly four sizes too big.

Lank, straight hair, glasses, an oversized sweater… God, I can already hear your thoughts! Everything you think about me. The way you think I think. I don't care! But stop, because I'm trying to tell you a story, my story, her story…If you're going to turn up your nose, just walk away now. I've suffered enough as it is, I'm through with suffering. If you turn up your nose at me it can't humiliate me any more than what I've already endured. Take your purity elsewhere, because this is an impure story. A dirty story. But it's important to me, and I'm going to tell the truth.

I was already vaguely in love with her even before the first time I saw her drinking tea. During orientation, she sat across from me, her slender arms withdrawn into her long, baggy sleeves like eels hidden in a coral reef. The flaccid sleeves were folded in her lap, except for when she occasionally used them to rub her eyes or nose. Then, without warning, her small, pale claws would emerge from the sleeves to pick up her phone and tap away it for several minutes, before setting the device back down in her lap and retracting once more into the safety of the navy blue cotton sweater emblazoned in white across the chest with the name of the private girl's college where, presumably, she had gone to school for computer science.

My background was in marketing, not computers, but because the company was small we wouldn't be shunted off into separate departments. We'd all be working together, more or less.

During orientation we all had to go around and share our name along with "two truths and a lie" as a way to break the ice and get to know one another. At the time, I missed her name, or failed to remember it later, but I remember distinctly her response to the "two truths and a lie" when it was her turn and the manager leading the orientation prompted her to speak.

Her hands came out of the sleeves, and even pushed them up past her wrists. Even though she wasn't using them, their emergence from the sweater signaled her presence and participation in public life.

"Um, let's see," she said. "I've been to France. I love cats. And I'm allergic to chocolate."

I was stunned. The flagrant mediocrity of her reply enchanted me, her refusal to be creative or "unique," her ease and professionalism in performing the bare minimum expediently, mathematically, surgically, like a student reciting the correct answer for the professor with zero enthusiasm and without a trace of irony. Though such a response was technically perfect and above reproach, her whole performance was nevertheless undergirded by a subtle and barely detectable narcissistic disregard, evident in the robotic manner of her alienated, detached expression and everything which it might possibly conceal, as well as from the sheer fact of her physical beauty, disguised as it was by the baggy sweater, long hair, and glasses. Her words floated on the surface of our collective reality like oil in a pool of water.

I decided to be infatuated with her, but only in the fleeting, harmless way that one sometimes falls in love with mysterious neighbors or strangers on the subway. Despite the fact that we would be working together, and I would doubtless have infinite opportunities to strike up a conversation or even ask her on a date, she nevertheless appeared in that moment so remote and inaccessible that I gave up from the beginning on ever even speaking to her. I resigned myself to an illusory passion, to admire her for a day or a week, to let the dream burn fast in my heart and then die.

Orientation lasted a few days, and then we settled into our new roles in the office. The company, or "start-up" as the owners liked to call it, was designing a software application for a company that designed software applications for Wall Street. The software application itself, as one of the owners revealed to the marketing team in a meeting, may in fact never be completed, but this didn't matter—the point wasn't to actually build the software, not really. The point was to build enough of it so that certain technological patents could be secured, and so that a certain aura of inevitability and dynamism could be cultivated around the "start-up" itself as a pioneering and "disruptive," even "revolutionary" presence in the sub-sub-field of software engineering which we occupied. The end goal, however, was the precise opposite of "disruption" and "revolution": at a certain, undefined point, the entire company was to be sold off to a larger company, possibly even to one of the tech monopolies or to an investment bank or hedge fund, so that they could obtain our patents. The owners would become millionaires, our "start-up" would be liquidated, and, if we were lucky, some of us might get to keep our jobs at the company which bought us out.

My job mainly consisted of writing press releases, manipulating online discourse, and researching ways to discredit our competitor, another "start-up" racing to develop parallel software which might render ours unnecessary. On an average day, I worked for about one or two hours, and spent the remaining time reading articles and short stories and scrolling through social media.

I couldn't remember her name, the girl with the sweater, but it just so happened—and you'll simply have to trust me when I assure you that I did not arrange this— that from my cubicle, and only mine, I could see her at an angle, from behind, whereas otherwise her back was to the wall. She had almost complete privacy, but if I peered over I could see her little hands peeking out of her long sleeves, her pink fingertips gliding and splashing over the plastic keys of her computer with expert speed and lucidity. I suppose she was writing or editing code, doing whatever it was that coders do, but I could see the edge of her computer screen and from the flashes of color I knew she was also often skimming blogs, social media, online stores. Next to her keyboard was a large steaming mug with the cotton string tail of a teabag dangling from its side.

I've had silent crushes on beautiful girls before, of course—quiet ones and strange ones in particular appealed to me because, I imagined, their silence betrayed a secret richness which haunted me and which like a mystic knight or sorcerer I craved. My most precious moments have always been within the worlds which the silence of beautiful women inspire. But nothing, nothing had ever terrified and obsessed me to the very core of my being like when I saw this girl dip her sleeve into her steaming cup, then suck the tea from her sweater like an infant, like a vampire, like a lunatic.

I was spying on her one day during that first week of work when I caught her. At first, I thought it was an accident. When she dunked her sleeve into the cup, I thought it was because she'd been reaching for something—a notepad, a pen, or for the handle of the mug itself—but, caught up in her work, she somehow mistakenly submerged the loose end of the sleeve into the tea.

But then she shook it, the sleeve, letting the excess liquid drip back into the cup, exactly as you would do with a biscuit that you'd dunked into coffee, tea, or milk.

It wasn't her college sweater, the one she'd worn in orientation. This was a ribbed turtleneck, striped with forest green, ocher, crimson, black, and gray. It hugged her body, but still, somehow, the sleeves were several sizes too long.

Her eyes remained fixed on the computer screen. She was utterly absorbed in whatever she was reading, which seemed to be a woman's fashion blog.

Absentmindedly, distractedly, she brought the sopping, loosely hanging bit of sleeve to her mouth, and sucked it.

The shock which ran through my spine was equal parts visceral repulsion and erotic fascination. I could not react, could not even think. I was in a trance of primordial captivation. And then I watched as she did it again.

Instantly, uncontrollably, and with overwhelming clarity I imagined the sensation: the exact texture and flavor of wet cotton, the warmth of the tea, the feeling of fabric sucking against teeth and tongue. I could imagine the way the sweater would have absorbed the taste of her skin, the fragrant sweat of her wrists, the dirt and grime of her hands. Or, if it was clean, the taste and smell of fresh laundry.

Despite my initial horror, it was all immensely satisfying, comforting, nostalgic. Though I had no memory of having done so—either in the moment or later when I racked my brain in an attempt to recall anything of the kind—it was as if I too had done this exact thing, or something quite like it, as a child.

I knew then that I was in love with her. Not in the common, flippant, though still magic way, of projecting one's fantasy onto the other. No, now I had seen, and felt, and tasted *her* fantasy, the most precious kind: the living, breathing fantasy of sensation.

The striped, ribbed turtleneck, the blue sweater with the white lettering of her college, and a crimson hoodie. These were the three baggy sweaters she cycled through, and from which she mopped and sucked Darjeeling tea with sugar and whole milk—always the left sleeve, always at her desk, always in secret (except, of course, for me).

At a certain point I decided I needed to see her making the tea, so I took some documents into the break room, slowly leafing through them and highlighting passages at random while I picked over the remains of a bagel. I pretended to remain preoccupied with my work even as she came in, rinsed out the electric kettle, filled it with fresh water, and flicked the plastic "On" switch, which then lit up with electric orange.

At that moment one of our insipid managers wafted into the break room and alighted on her, launching into a stream of meaningless talk. "I wanted to remind you…" Can't you see she doesn't need to be reminded? Her mind is perfect without you. Anyway, something tells me that while, yes, you *wanted* to remind her, you didn't really believe that you *needed* to remind her. But while all of our activity in this office was, at a certain level, fraudulent and meaningless, this was above all true for the managers, who perhaps out of an acute awareness of their own uselessness, compensated by constantly busying themselves with the work of "managing," which consisted almost entirely of "reminding" the workers of things they never needed to know in the first place, and probably would have been better off never having been told.

Meanwhile, I admired her—the girl who sucked tea from her sweater—her way of crossing her arms and smiling vacantly at this verbal effluvium spewing from the lips of the manager. I admired her, and yet, in that moment, I realized that if I ever tried to speak with her, to strike up a conversation, or ask her out on a date, she would probably just smile and nod at me in the exact same way…Probably, she saw me the same way she saw the manager and everyone else in the office. After all, I was in marketing. She would assume I was like all the rest. Certainly, I behaved outwardly and dressed like they did. The plaid blazer, which I often wore and which at that very moment I had on—she probably thought it was flashy and imbecilic, if she even noticed it at all. I suddenly wanted to burn it.

I took this job because I needed the money, just like her. But she must have thought she was better off from a spiritual standpoint, because her work was strictly technical, while mine was aesthetically and morally compromised. She probably imagined that I as a person was compromised, that my plaid blazer, my designer shoes, my face, my past experiences, my dreams, my capacity for love, all was compromised, and probably she was right. I'd been placed in a series of compromising positions for my entire life, culminating in a profession which I despised and which I despised myself for doing. She probably imagined that I was compromised but she was not, because due to the nature of her work she could maintain a complete separation from the job and her life, and the mystery and treasure of life she kept alive like a secret flame guarded from year to year since childhood. No parent, boyfriend, or psychiatrist had broken her. She was in possession of the most delicate thing in the world which is also the most indestructible. She had it, and I did not.

The electric kettle began to boil, automatically switched itself off. The orange light of the "On" switch died, and the girl who sucked tea from her sweater, still smiling vacantly, turned her body toward the kettle while still keeping her face fixed on the supervisor, as a way of indicating a contradiction which must soon be resolved. The canny supervisor got the hint and, with a final "reminder," drifted away in search of fresh prey.

I've always loved the sound of boiling water being poured into a ceramic cup, quickly followed by the perfume of ground tea leaves absolving into the atmosphere. I didn't particularly enjoy drinking tea, but the ritual of it was comforting, satisfying—probably because I'd witnessed my mother performing these actions, discharging these sounds and smells into the world, every morning and night for the decade and a half of my conscious childhood and adolescence. Was this why I'd camped out in the break room like a private detective, hoping to witness the ritual of tea brewing, in order to turn this girl, the girl who sucked tea from her sweater, into my mother?

The paper tag stapled to the cotton string on the teabag had been accidentally sucked into the mug by the force of the cascading water. She now had to pick it out with her fingernails and flick it over the side of the mug, where, damp and limp, it became plastered to the ceramic. Next, she opened two packets of sugar from the communal basket of coffee supplies, ripped them open, and poured them in with the tea.

She was wearing her crimson hoodie (which was so long that it reached her mid-thigh), black leggings, and white tennis shoes. Bending shapelessly like a worm, she reached into the refrigerator and withdrew a carton of milk.

My entire conception of Freud had been absorbed secondhand in college. I tried to recall what an oral fixation was, but quickly decided that I didn't care. She poured the milk. She stirred the tea. Darjeeling tea should be steeped for three to five minutes at 205 degrees Fahrenheit, not stirred in boiling water and left to sit and become bitter from over-steeping. But then again, it is also meant to be sipped from a mug or teacup, not soaked into and nursed out of the sleeve of a woman's sweater.

Before I knew it, she had already left the breakroom with her tea. What was I doing? What was my plan? It was Friday. Soon it would be the weekend and I wouldn't get to see her again for two days, during which time I would lay around my apartment, drink, blow some of my paycheck on online gambling, maybe read a novel, but mostly dream about her.

The next week brought major news in the office which, while seeming at first to be, like everything else announced by the company's owners, radically uninteresting and irrelevant, later proved to be of profound and irreversible consequence, nothing short of a catastrophe.

A journalist from the business press, we were told, was doing a profile on the company's owners, who were to be included in a new list of promising young tech entrepreneurs. This reporter would be making a visit to the company office, which must appear as a reflection of its creators' youthful genius and dynamism. But there was a problem—the office was neither ingenious nor dynamic, not in the slightest. It was quite the ordinary office, consisting of gray paneled cubicles, white walls, the drone of computers and the clacking of keyboards. This would not do. Rapid and far-reaching changes had to be wrought in a short amount of time. The owners scrambled to rethink the company "culture" and "social architecture" in order to better showcase their "radical" leadership style. I myself was taken off my regular duties to help research trends and buzzwords for the office redesign, which had to be executed in a matter of days.

Soon, the plans had been drawn by members of the marketing and graphic design teams (a professional decorator having been decided to be too expensive) and signed off on by the owners, who announced to the company that they had designed the new office themselves. With deadlines approaching, it wasn't possible to give us any extra time off, so we had to keep working while the contractors tore down and reconstructed the office around us, and the movers brought in the new furniture. It was finished in three days.

The embarrassingly outdated cubicles were destroyed. The new layout, intended to be more "open" and "collaborative," consisted of various shared tables and sofas, so that our office now resembled a coffee shop catering to bohemians and college students. The wall separating the break room from the rest of the office had been knocked down. The harsh fluorescent lighting had been softened, and the walls painted a calming pale yellow like in a psychiatric ward or hospice, and decorated with vintage music concert posters, abstract paintings, and framed quotations from Ralph Waldo Emerson, David Bowie, etc. Taps had been installed with free cold coffee and expensive "craft" beer, along with a basket of fresh pastries that was to be replenished each morning from a nearby bakery.

Work was work, and personally I didn't care how they decorated it. Despite the owners' self-congratulatory speech about the redesign, in which they tried to get the office excited about the new arrangement, no one else seemed to care very much either, except for the handful of people keen on free alcohol. In the beginning, I was so swept up in helping plan the whole thing, and then distracted by the hustle and bustle of the contractors, that the obvious consequence of the new "social architecture" had completely failed to occur to me. It was only the next day, when the journalist was slated to arrive for his tour and interview with the owners, and I was beginning to settle back into my normal routine of work, that it dawned on me what we had done.

I chose one of the few one-person tables where I could sit with my back to the wall. I was pretending to work, skimming through my social media feed and sipping coffee, when I idly glanced over at her, the girl who sucked tea from her sweater. Having made a fresh cup of tea, she had just returned to her place, curled up on a loveseat in her striped ribbed turtleneck, a laptop computer balanced on her knee, the white screen reflected in her glasses, the steaming cup of tea held in the delicate hands protruding from the bunched-up sleeves.

She blew away the steam, waited for the tea to cool. And then she sipped the tea. Sipped it from the mug, just like anyone would else would do.

I inhaled sharply. My veins turned to ice. What had I done?

It was over. I'd never see her suck tea from her sweater again…Of course she'd never do it like this, out in the open, in a "collaborative workspace." Without cubicles, without privacy…

"This is it. We call it the *study room*. We designed it ourselves."

The two owners had just emerged from the building corridor with a stranger, presumably the journalist, who was holding out a microphone to capture every detail of their obscene pablum as they began to walk through the "study room" toward the executive office in the back.

"We don't think of this place as a traditional company. We're more like a cross between a bohemian café, an art studio, and a NASA laboratory."

"It's a gymnasium," cut in the other genius, "for exercising the *mind*."

I put on a pair of headphones, turned the volume up loud, closed my browser windows, and stared at the blank, black background on my computer for a good, long hour.

Weeks went by.

I had seen something no one was supposed to see. I had seen behind the veil. I had glimpsed the feral life which is the secret origin of all life. I knew that it would haunt me for a long time, possibly for the rest of my days. But there was nothing that could be done.

I suppose it was this fatalistic and dejected attitude which attracted her attention. She must have seen something of herself reflected in me for the first time, because one day, while I was still in the depths of my dark mood, it was she who came to me…

"You look like you need a drink."

That's what she said to me. I couldn't believe it. I'd been gazing into my sandwich, thinking about nothing, when she spoke these words. She sat down next to me with the piece of fruit she was eating for lunch. We talked briefly, introduced ourselves. It was the first time we'd ever exchanged words. At the end of three minutes we had agreed to meet for drinks after work.

I was in a daze of wild hope and angst for the rest of the afternoon. I couldn't believe that she'd noticed me. What did it mean? Did we have a future? Was it possible that one day I could see her again, the real her?

After work we walked together to a dive bar a few blocks from the office. We drank and talked about work, politics, books. Just the other day she'd caught me with a paperback of one of her favorite novelists—so that was it. She invited me back to her apartment. I ran my hands along the outside of her sweater, I watched her pull it over her head.

All of this occurred last year. We've been living together now for three months. Things are going quite well. We make dinner together, we cuddle on the sofa and watch television. The sex is fantastic, and with her next to me in bed I sleep better than any other point in my life. In so many ways, we're each different than how we expected the other to be. I still feel like I'm learning who she is. And I love her more and more each day and week. We have created our own private world away from work, away from the eyes and ears, the hands and mouths of the human race.

The problem is the tea…I make it for her, in the evenings, on the weekends…Why won't she drink it the way she used to? Her shyness has dissolved. She's come out of her shell. She walks around the apartment completely naked. She talks openly and curses like a sailor. She lets me do whatever I want to her in bed. She loves me, she trusts me, I know she does. Why won't she drink the tea like she used to?

She must feel my eyes on her at all times. Perhaps she does it, in fact I'm sure she must, whenever I'm not around. Or does she? Perhaps she's grown out of it? Did something change? Did something click? Is it me?

Perhaps in the future there could be clubs, parties, orgies where people suck on cotton sleeves with wild abandon. Yes, it's all possible, perhaps it's even already going on, and perhaps it would be immensely liberating, satisfying, and beautiful, but would it be the same? Even if I could find it somewhere, I wouldn't want it. I only want her. I want her secret to be mine. I want her shame to be ours.

My dream—that she would wear one of her baggy sweaters, and nothing else, that we would embrace, that we would drink tea, together…with each day I'm less and less sure it will ever be possible, that I will ever be able to coax it out of her.

I couldn't ask. I couldn't even hint at it. I know she would be humiliated, She would withdraw back into her shell, into her sweater. Perhaps I could fall to my knees and beg her, kiss her feet, promise her everything, confess everything, lay bare my fantasy and beg for mercy. But what if it all went wrong? Shame, disgust, betrayal…I can't risk that. I can't risk the love we've found. And so, I wait…

I hope, but this hope is making me sick. Should I surrender to ordinary love? Ordinary happiness?

I fear that something delicate has been lost, and I'll never forgive the world for that. Then again, it was this world, or some version of it, which in the first place provided the soil, the sun, the water, for her secret flower to grow.

Will I glimpse it again? Ever again?

Even when I touch her skin, when I whisper to her, penetrate her, I am miles away, I am in another world. I fear I will never be with her truly until we are together in this way.

I have no choice but to wait and to pray for her to reveal herself. With the subtlest invitations, I kneel to her.

My love, please…Share yourself with me.

SCREAM DRINKER

You have heard the strangled cries of dreamers—haven't you wondered why the scream always fails to escape their throats? Perhaps you've been there, in a nightmare whose horror is unspeakable, horror which would appear supremely childish and absurd in the light of day, but which in the darkness dominates you absolutely.

When you gaze upon the face of evil, or feel its fingers grossly clinging to your shirt or your limbs, and you scream with all your might—not a playful squeal, not a yelp of surprise, not a groan of pain—but a scream of mortal panic and fear, the deep instinct of survival bursting out from your heart and your lungs, a scream that says, without words: *Help me. Someone, anyone. You must come now and help me. I am in danger. I, or someone I love, is going to die. Someone, anyone. If you can hear this, you must come help me now.*

You squeeze your lungs, you open your throat and your lips, but nothing comes out, nothing but a muffled, senile moan which nobody can hear. And if nobody can hear it, then nobody can help you, nobody *will* help you. You are alone in your utmost fear, alone in your primeval witness of death. Nobody is coming to save you.

What happened to your scream? It was taken by Her. Devoured by Her. Consumed by Her. She drinks screams like water. She sucks them from your mouth like kisses, like ejaculations which she lusts for insatiably.

She climbs through your window, her limbs like spider legs, angular and wicked, searching, invading, subjugating your bedroom in the darkness. Her hair falls black and thick, dragging behind her, pooling in mystic eddies on the floor.

She is red with fever. She presses herself against your writhing body, suffocating your skin with her burning heat, enrapturing you, ushering you into nightmares, driving you like a frightened animal into her fold.

When your scream comes, she is there to swallow it all. The freezing ice of your scream turns to hissing vapor in her fiery throat, intoxicating her, as she crushes your lungs, squeezing them dry.

In the moment before you awaken, she falls back, reclining on the sweat-dampened mattress, her eyes glazed over, losing focus, her jaw hanging open in a drunken smile dripping with spit. And then she is gone.

Defiled, you awaken, and perhaps you weep, drink a cup of tea, read a book, hold a lover in your arms, and pray for dreamless oblivion when you shut your eyes again.

While you slave away, bored and angry and tired in the cruel light of day, She sleeps, perfectly contented, smiling and dreaming in her palace of shadows and pain.

THE FRIDGE

"I want to get in her *fridge*."

Pete bit his lip as he leered at the woman, not without some measure of ironic self-awareness. Mackenzie giggled, shaking his head in pretend disapproval.

Ivan was confused. "Her fridge?"

"Yeah, man," said Pete. "Haven't I told you about fridging?"

"Here we go," groaned Mackenzie, clearly loving it.

"I don't know what that is," confessed Ivan.

They were sitting in a booth in the back corner of the shadowy bar, stealing glances at the woman with the army jacket and combat boots and long black hair that fell past her shoulders straight as a knife's edge.

Pete adjusted himself in his seat, suppressing a smug grin as he settled in for his lecture.

"Ivan," he said, "have you ever been talking to a woman, and it seems like things are going really well, but she's always 'too busy' to hang out, and you get the sense that she's avoiding you?"

"Yes," admitted Ivan.

"And? What's your response in that situation?"

"Well, I assume she's not interested after all, but she's just being polite, so she says she's busy. Eventually, I get the message and I stop trying to ask her out."

Pete snapped his fingers, then pointed aggressively at Ivan. "Boom. There's your mistake. When that happens, she's not just being polite. Chances are she really *is* busy. Busy with other guys."

For a moment, Ivan thought that he was being made fun of, and he scowled into his glass of beer. Beside him, Mackenzie was still bemusedly shaking his head.

"You see," Pete went on, his gaze lifting up toward the ceiling as he basked in the justice and elegance of his theory, "guys like us will never be a beautiful woman's first choice. The fact is, she can do better. She *does* do better. But our situation is not hopeless. We may not be her first choice, but we may very well be a serviceable third, fourth, or even fifth choice…But in order to get to that point, we have to get comfortable with the fridge."

"I'm lost," said Ivan impatiently. "What's the fridge?"

"It's where you put food to keep it fresh," offered Mackenzie helpfully. "You don't want to eat it yet, but you're keeping it for later."

"The fridge," explained Pete, now leaning in candidly, "is exactly where you want to be. When she is disappointed, bored, exasperated with her first, second, and third choice, *that's* when she comes to you—in a state of desperation. That is exactly where you want to be. The last man standing. Slow and steady wins the race."

"Tortoise and the hair," put in Mackenzie, shaking his head as if won over to the wisdom of Pete's argument despite his own reservations.

"Exactly," said Pete. "And just like the tortoise, you have to have a thick skin."

"Don't you mean a shell?" countered Ivan doubtfully.

"Whatever. The point is, you need to be able to deal with rejection. If it's a hard rejection, then you're out, you've been thrown to the curb. But a soft rejection? The 'I'm just busy this week' line? That's the fridge. You have to bide your time. *Stay cool.* And when she's ready, when she's *hungry*, she'll come looking…for an easy snack."

Finally, Mackenzie's horizontal head-shaking turned to a vertical nod. The genius of Pete's vision could no longer be denied. Even Ivan's skepticism had now melted into quiet contemplation of the past and future, soberly reconsidered now in the framework of this new theory.

"And now," said Pete, riding high on the success of his disquisition, "we put it to the test."

The woman with the army jacket and combat boots and long, straight black hair, whose name was Amelia, was not a stranger to Pete, Mackenzie, and Ivan, but nor was she a friend. They moved in overlapping circles, shared mutual acquaintances, frequented the same bars (namely, this one). Mackenzie's roommate Nick was Amelia's co-worker, and had raved before about the unusual but excellent cooking that she often brought in to the office.

Pete had met her more than once before, at parties thrown at Mackenzie and Nick's apartment. He had always thought she was odd, but there was something about her that drew him in. Now, on the pretense of going to the bar for a fresh round of drinks, he made his move.

Ivan and Mackenzie, clutching their glasses containing the dregs of now room-temperature beer, watched apprehensively as Pete approached the bar, flagged down the bartender, then pretended to notice Amelia for the first time. They chatted amiably, he made her laugh, and then they both took out their phones…

"You got her number?" asked Mackenzie when Pete returned to the table with three full pints of cold beer.

"That's the easy part," said Pete modestly. "We were just being friendly. No firm commitments. The question is, when I text her later to ask her out—will she throw me to the dogs, or will she make space for me in that sweet, sweet fridge?"

"What if she just says 'yes'?" asked Ivan.

Pete and Mackenzie glared at him blankly.

Casually, in a way that was both offhand and direct, Pete asked Amelia to get a drink with him. She explained that she was busy, so he waited, and the next week asked her the same thing. Again, she declined—she just had too much going on.

Several weeks passed like this. In the interim, Pete hung out with Mackenzie and Ivan, assuring them that everything was going exactly to plan, that she hadn't really rejected him, that she was just keeping him on ice, keeping him in the fridge.

As for Amelia, according to Nick she was with a different guy every week, if not every night. It seemed that Pete had indeed picked the perfect woman to test out his theory—someone out of his league, but only just slightly, who wouldn't take him as her first choice but who would go through other guys fast enough that his turn might eventually come. And sure enough, it did.

Pete gloated (in a self-aware, ironic way). Everything had been confirmed. Mackenzie and Ivan never would have dared to ask Amelia out in the first place, and even if they would have tried it, they, like the average self-respecting person, would have given up after two or three weeks of excuses, cancellations, and lackluster texts. But Pete stuck with it, until five weeks had passed, and finally Amelia set a date with him that she did not cancel.

"She must be desperate," Pete muttered, half to his friends and half to himself, his eyes misty with fantasies. He was at the bar with Mackenzie and Ivan the night before the date.

"We'll see," said Mackenzie with exaggerated mock jealousy. "She still has time to cancel again."

Ivan, for whom fridging had thus far born no fruit, concealed his jealousy the old-fashioned way. "Good luck," he said bitterly.

Amelia was neither tall nor short, neither ugly nor beautiful, neither forward nor shy, neither mousy nor hip. Hers was an entirely ambiguous character. Adding to this uncertainty was the ambivalence of her ethnicity, with her pallid face and vague features suggesting various possibilities. The long, straight black hair that fell past her shoulders, the large, square-framed glasses, and the delicate flourish of acne on the ridge of her cheeks—all this served to further obscure any general impression that one might make, almost as if she were wearing a disguise. And yet, somehow, even without a distinct sense of what she actually looked like, the overall effect was arresting. Maybe she wasn't beautiful, or *hot*, exactly—but for someone like Pete, especially, there was no doubt that she was alluring.

She was wearing her army jacket and combat boots again, just like the night that Pete had lectured Mackenzie and Ivan on the merits of fridging. And she was sitting on the exact same stool in the same bar. When Pete entered the bar and approached her at the appointed time, she presented him with a tight-lipped smile, then said: "Hello."

"What are you drinking?"

"Vodka cranberry."

"Another round, please," said Pete to the bartender, drawing a decisive circle in the air with his index finger.

Pete and Amelia had several vodka cranberries. They talked about work, television, pets—ordinary stuff. But all the while, Pete could feel Amelia's eyes on him. She was sizing him up. She pouted her lips as she checked out his biceps, his legs, his chest, and smiled as she gazed into his eyes, clearly not paying attention to his words but forming judgments about his intelligence, his style, his jawline.

Pete could almost read her mind. Her thoughts were written in her face. *He'll do.*

"I'll be honest," she said at one point while they were discussing dating. "Most of the guys I hook up with, it's just about sex."

Pete shrugged and smirked as if he too were having plenty of casual sex, and that it was really no big deal.

"But what I'm really looking for," Amelia went on, making intense, unblinking eye contact with Pete, "is something…special."

"Oh?" said Pete, completely taken off guard by this confession. He tried to keep looking blasé and collected, but his heart was pounding so hard he was afraid she'd hear it.

"Yes," said Amelia, breaking eye contact suddenly to look off into space. "I had someone else, but I'm finished with him now. Or I will be, after tonight."

Pete opened his mouth but was unable to say anything. He covered up his bafflement by taking a sip of his vodka cranberry, even though all that was left now was red-stained ice.

"Do you want to see my apartment?" said Amelia suddenly. "It's close by."

Pete cleared his throat. "Yes," he replied, all measure of ironic self-awareness now fled from his demeanor. "I'd like that very much."

Amelia smoked a cigarette on the way back to her apartment, so that when they kissed, standing in her kitchen, her mouth tasted like cheap tobacco. Pete loved it, and it made him wonder if she liked the taste of him.

He placed his hands on her hips, beneath the fabric of her shirt, touching her warm skin, pulling her close to him. He'd been in the cold for so long, all he wanted was to feel that warmth, even if it was just for one night.

The smugness and thrill of his victory had completely melted away. Pete was innocent, vulnerable, overwhelmed by a surge of tender emotion. He was so absorbed in the moment that he didn't notice Amelia holding the kitchen knife until she gently broke away from their kiss, placing one hand on Pete's chest, and using the other to plunge the knife into the base of his throat.

Pete opened his mouth but was unable to say anything. All he could do was gasp for air, as if he just needed to catch his breath and recover from the initial shock, and then, when he was ready, he could respond appropriately to the fact that a blade was pierced six inches deep in his throat. But he never got the chance.

Amelia had pushed the knife at a downward angle right above Pete's sternum. She was trembling all over, her eyes wide with manic glee as she suddenly twisted the blade, slashing Pete's esophagus and trachea. Dark blood gushed from his lips, all over the knife blade and Amelia's hands. She let go, allowing him to stumble backwards, and then, for Pete, everything became suddenly dark.

Had he been her first?

According to Nick, she was with a different guy every week, if not every night. Certainly, she couldn't be doing this to all of them. She'd be found out. Was it only a select few, then? Or was it only one, only Pete? Did she choose him? Was he special?

These were the thoughts which filled Pete's dim mind as he awoke in the darkness. He was weak, and cold, sitting propped upright in some kind of box or closet. It hurt to breathe, but he could still get air into his lungs.

Pete knew he was dying, and he knew from watching movies that dying made you feel cold. But this was different. The walls of the closet were cold, the air was cold…

He could hear something outside. Amelia's voice, speaking, sighing…

Lifting a trembling hand, he pressed it against the plastic door of his closet and pushed. Though nearly all his strength was depleted, and the door was held fast by a rubber lip that clung to the plastic doorframe, he was able to push it open.

Light flooded into the world as his bloody hand fell away from the door, smearing it with red. He was in Amelia's kitchen. The smell of cooked meat reached his nostrils. Spaghetti bolognese?

From where he sat (inside of the refrigerator, he now realized), he could see the dinner table, where Amelia was bent over the remains of the meal, while a man took her from behind, squeezing her warm hips while he thrust inside of her. Her eyes shut, her glasses askew on her nose, Amelia shuddered and sighed.

Pete remembered then what Amelia had said. She had sex with plenty of men, but Pete was different, he was special. But he wasn't her first. There had been another, someone before him. But after tonight, she said, she'd be finished with him. The bolognese…

The refrigerator door swung slowly back toward Pete. He was powerless to stop it from shutting him in the darkness and cold again. The last thing he saw was the white fog of his own ragged breath, before the door shut and everything was black.

"She'll come for me," he whispered feebly through lips caked with dried blood. "When he leaves in the morning, she'll be hungry…and then she'll come for me at last…"

MY FORGOTTEN SUMMER

Millie cut the engine and the music abruptly stopped.

"I don't want you to be nervous," said Eliza. "My dad likes you." In the sudden gloom and hermetic silence of the parked car, each word was sticky and close. She shifted slightly, and the sound of her nylon coat on the fabric of the car seat was so intimate and real that it woke Millie up from her daydream, and she reached out and touched Eliza's hand.

"It's not him I'm worried about," said Millie. "Half the department is going to be there."

"So what? They'll all be impressed with you. Just be yourself. I love you."

"I love you too."

They kissed, synthetic polymers rustling in the half-light.

"Come in, come in!"

Eliza's father, Dr. Lesley Ross, ushered them inside, into the vast golden warmth of the Victorian house. He embraced Eliza and gave a Millie a handshake. He was a large, gentle, bear-like man, who moved with constant hesitations and doubletakes, frequently squinting through his thick glasses and smoothing his thick gray mustache with his rough fingers.

"There's food on the table and drinks in the kitchen. Everyone is in the living room."

"Okay Dad."

Dr. Ross shuffled away while Eliza and Millie took off their shoes and coats. The foyer was stuffed with bulky winter coats and a pile of boots. Millie always found that it took her longer than anyone else to remove her shoes. She was only finishing the first boot when Eliza grew impatient.

"I'm going to say hi to people. I'll meet you in the kitchen, okay?"

"Okay," Millie gasped for air as she pulled off her boot. As she set to work unlacing the second one, she became increasingly, uncomfortably warm. In the sudden heat of the house, her quilted parka—over a flannel shirt, a thermal undershirt, and an elastic chest binder—was far too much. She considered pausing to remove the parka, but it occurred to her that someone might witness her doing this. A guest returning to the foyer to fetch something from the pocket of a coat, or perhaps stepping outside to smoke a cigarette or take a phone call inside a car, might stumble upon Millie pausing with one boot off and the other still on but half-unlaced, in the process of removing her coat, a totally awkward position.

By the time Millie yanked off her second boot, she was sweating. She placed her boots carefully next to the others, on top of the absorbent mat that was already wet with melted snow. Then she removed her coat. Each hook on the coat rack was already occupied by two or three cumbrous parkas or overcoats. On the bench next to where Millie had sat to unlace her boots there was a growing heap of coats. She placed hers on top of this slippery pile, which was already in danger of cascading over onto the assemblage of wet boots.

Every room in the Ross house was on a slightly different level. To move from one room to the next involved stepping up or down one or several steps. Stepping up out of the shadowy foyer, one found oneself in a long, narrow golden corridor leading to the dining room and the kitchen. The chatter of voices and music radiated from the living room on the other side of the dining area.

The feeling of walking with socks on clean, slippery hardwood floors, leading into the kitchen tile, reminded Millie of being a kid in her parents' house. For years she'd been living in tiny apartments where there were no long hallways, places where the kitchen tile is so old and warped, and the space so cramped, that there was nowhere to slip around the same way.

Across the dining room table was an extravagant spread of *hors d'oeuvres*. It had already sustained the initial and most ferocious wave of depredations, but there was still plenty of food. At risk of being noticed by anyone in the adjacent living room, Millie hurried into the kitchen, which was thankfully empty. Pouring herself a glass of red wine from one of the many open bottles on the countertop, she heard the voice behind her.

"Millie! How are you?"

Eliza's mother, Eleanor, smiled painfully as she entered the kitchen.

"I'm good, how are you?"

"Listen, I'm not going to allow you to hide in the kitchen. Come on now, I'm going to introduce you to James and Julie."

The living room was packed with bodies. Innocuous, quite ordinary but oddly unclassifiable music was piped in through a system of speakers positioned discretely behind potted plants and nestled in bookshelves: guitar, clarinet, brush on snare drum, a woman singing hoarsely. It was played at such a volume as to remain only barely perceptible above the murmur of conversation.

Eleanor led Millie to where Eliza and her father were talking to James and Julie Ford. They taught poetics in the department, and had been like an aunt and uncle to Eliza. Eleanor made the introductions and Millie shook their hands in turn.

"And what pronouns do you use?" asked Julie Ford. Her gray curls, bunched in a loose ponytail, fell to one side as she cocked her head and looked expectantly at Millie.

Millie opened her mouth but nothing came out. Everyone was staring at her. She cleared her throat. Julie's smile slowly turned into a grimace, her lips peeling back over her teeth as her nose shriveled. James Ford muttered something inaudible and took a sip of his wine. One by one, gazes broke away, and the web of concentration was broken. Lesley went on speaking as if nothing had happened.

"Millie is one of our most promising young writers," he proclaimed.

"Are you a poet?" asked James politely, offering her an easy question.

"Sort of," Millie laughed nervously, pushing her glasses up the bridge of her nose. "No. Well, not exactly."

Julie Ford had not yet succeeded in wiping the distaste from her countenance. She was forced to hide her face by becoming suddenly interested in the potted fern behind her.

James furrowed his brow but smiled generously. Eleanor came to the rescue.

"So, Eliza," she said, addressing not Eliza but everyone in the group, "your father has finally finished the spare room. You know, he's been working on that room since before you moved out."

Lesley waved away the accomplishment modestly with one of his large paws. At this moment, James gestured decisively with his wine glass, as if stamping out the memory of his interactions with Millie with the base of the glass, and began quizzing Lesley on his carpentry hobby, a subject completely impenetrable to Millie. With everyone mercifully ignoring her, she drifted away.

Eliza caught up with her. "Hey. Are you having fun?"

"Yes, of course."

"I'm sorry about Julie," Eliza whispered.

"It's fine, really."

"Go meet some people. You're doing great!"

Millie refilled her wine glass in the kitchen before returning to the party. There were exactly four other graduate students in attendance, and they were all clustered around the visiting writer. There seemed to be no openings in the living room, and so she retreated to the adjoining library which was also filled with people. Glancing around for an opportunity, she suddenly found herself enlisted.

"Millie, how are you?"

It was Dennis Gray, a major personality in the department. He taught a notorious seminar on literary theory, which Millie had so far avoided, but they had briefly met previously at a department event. Millie wasn't tall, but Dr. Gray was slightly shorter than her. His graying black hair was swept neatly to one side, his black beard speckled with gray. He wore square-frame glasses, a gray sweater over a white collared shirt, and black denim pants. He was constantly smiling and blinking.

"I was just talking with Andy about music. You're into punk rock, isn't that right?"

Andy was a lecturer from the philosophy department. He licked his lips distractedly, acutely aware that he had lost his monopoly on Dennis's attention.

"Yes," said Millie. Her mouth was suddenly dry, but she made up for it by drinking deeply from her glass.

"So what's your opinion," said Dennis. "What's Victimhood's best album?"

He smiled, but his eyes watched her coldly, calculating. Millie felt keenly that she was being somehow evaluated, though it was not clear why. But this was an easy question.

"*Losing Streak*," she said, without hesitating.

"Ah. Not *Dreaming of Dead Fish*?"

"*Dreaming of Dead Fish* is a great album. But *Losing Streak* is something else. It's perfect."

"Yes," said Dennis idly. He seemed to be chewing something over.

Andy tried to re-insert himself into the conversation by launching into some feeble anecdote, but Dennis had already pivoted decisively to Millie. He turned his head slightly to register what Andy was saying, then replied with a politely appreciative but dismissive grunt, before speaking again to Millie.

"So I take it you like other bands from that period. Sick Room, for example."

"Ah, Sick Room!" Andy gasped, wincing and waving his beer bottle.

Dennis glanced patiently at Andy before turning his gaze back to Millie.

"Yes, they're pretty good," she said, feeling pressured to respond positively. But this was a trap. Dennis clicked his tongue.

"I disagree," he said flatly. It was like he had been holding something back, and now he laid his card on the table with supreme satisfaction. "Not just because the songwriting is so derivative, but the whole self-pitying nostalgia trip…I can't get behind it."

At this moment the visiting writer appeared, apparently having slipped away from his admirers in the other room. He was tall, maybe 6'6. Faded tattoos crept out from the sleeves of his blazer, down his wrists and onto the top of his hands, curling around his fingers along with his collection of silver rings. The hand cupping his wine glass was adorned in rings, one of which contained a small red stone. Tattoos of ghosts and flowers covered his neck, thorns crept up behind one ear. His head was bald, a stripe of gray ran through his beard. He had the look of a barbarian warlord who, having triumphed in a career of pillage and assassination, learned how to assimilate to the civilization he spent his youth conquering, dressing and acting like a gentleman in order to enjoy his fame and money in an early retirement. Millie could not remember his name, but there was a high probability that it was Stanley.

"Talking about music?" he said.

"Oh, no, nothing," said Dennis, smiling. "Just grad school."

He said this last phrase as if to dismiss his entire exchange with Millie as mere trivialities, despite his obvious investment in it moments ago. Now he turned his attention fully to Stanley, but before he was able to engage him, Millie spoke. Emboldened by the alcohol, and by her refusal to be so easily humiliated, she found a stream of improvised phraseology ready at her lips which spilled forth without much thought.

"I don't think Sick Room is just nostalgic," she said. "They take this raw anguish and alienation and turn it into something truly poetic. That's the kind of work that defined the whole period. I think it's gothic and strange and beautiful."

Dennis turned and glared at her, his cheeks reddening, his eyes wide with the shock of betrayal.

Stanley nodded enthusiastically. "Yeah, I think I agree with you. Have you listened to Kill House?"

Clearly horrified, but unable to stem the exchange, Dennis looked on with mounting impatience, twice running his hand through his hair angrily as Millie discussed the merits of Kill House with Stanley. Andy remained hovering nearby, occasionally glancing around as if searching for help. And then quite naturally, not thinking anything of it, Millie mentioned Artificial Flowers.

Dennis blushed, his nostrils flaring with rage, his eyes darkening. Stanley recoiled softly, as if suddenly half-recalling some distant but poignant memory. His eyes wandered the bookshelves and the ceiling.

"Artificial Flowers, yes," he said, unconvincingly. "Yes, yes, of course."

Millie could not recall having returned to the kitchen to refill her cup, but she realized suddenly that she was quite drunk and must have consumed several glasses of wine. Taking advantage of the stunned silence, she glanced at her phone—it was past 11pm. Apparently, she'd somehow been at the party for over two hours.

It was then that Eleanor appeared. She touched Dennis's arm and said, "We're going to look at the spare room. Lesley has finally finished it."

Dennis nodded. "You know, sometimes," he remarked offhandedly, to no one in particular, "students try to 'friend' me on social media, but of course that's ridiculous. We're not friends."

"I don't have social media," said Millie flatly.

Dennis scowled, then turned away abruptly, ushering Stanley along with him. Eleanor glared at Millie. "Can I get you anything, Millie? A *glass of water*, perhaps?"

Having made her point, Eleanor turned away without waiting for a reply.

The whole party, it seemed, was now being led toward the stairs to ascend in search of the finished spare room. Millie followed sheepishly behind as people crowded through doorways from room to room.

"You know, Lesley did everything by hand," whispered someone in a chastising tone, as if being forced to state openly certain obvious facts which should have gone without saying. "He's quite the craftsman. But on account of his age, of course, he must pace himself."

"Yes," replied someone else pityingly. "He's been working on that spare room for years."

Millie stood on her tip-toes, peering over the heads and shoulders of the crowd. She spotted the back of Eliza's head, her blonde hair was like an aura of light. But there was no way to signal her, and she drifted farther and farther away.

The truth was that Millie hadn't thought about, or listened to, Artificial Flowers in many years. After a brief but violent romance with their first album, *My Forgotten Summer*, she'd abruptly moved on, but now the memories associated with the music became suddenly visible like patterns appearing in the grain of wood.

The crowd of guests moved through the living room and dining room, to the base of the stairs in the corridor. Eleanor was in front, leading the expedition that was now tramping up the creaking stairs. Halfway up, she leaned over the polished wooden banister.

"Lesley has finally finished the spare room!" she proclaimed. Beaming, she brushed away a strand of gray hair that was plastered to her sweaty face.

This must have been announced previously, because everyone was already crowding toward the stairs en masse, but as if hearing the revelation for the first time the assembled guests gasped and scoffed with admiring disbelief at this stunning triumph. Many of them repeated Eleanor's words to each other. The grad students in particular were eager to express their amazement, even those who did not know Dr. Ross and had only been in the program for three months.

The stairs groaned under the weight of the trudging guests as they ascended. Some leaned over the banister to catch a breath of fresh air or wave enthusiastically to those still below. Because many of the guests were advanced in years, the trek up the stairs required considerable exertion in the warm corridor which was increasingly humid from the presence of so many people.

The slanting, discordant melodies of *My Forgotten Summer*, the ideas which pierce the atmosphere at improbable and startling angles, were for Millie's memory enmeshed completely with the colors and textures of the album artwork—the velvet green banks, giving way to horizons of yellow ochre. Millie slipped away from the press of sweating bodies into the kitchen, rinsed out her wineglass in the sink and filled it with water.

"Aren't you going to look at the spare room?" It was Julie Ford, sticking her head into the kitchen and furrowing her brow at Millie. "Lesley's finally finished it."

"I was just getting some water," explained Millie.

Julie disappeared back into the congested pack, which had made some progress in funneling out of the corridor and onto the stairs. Overhead, Millie could hear the groaning floors, footsteps, and the jovial laughs and cries of acclaim as the first witnesses beheld the spare room.

The kitchen was connected to a dark, unused drawing room, which for some reason the party had not populated, crowding instead into the other living room and library. Millie turned on a light.

On the buffet loomed a large porcelain vase painted with bright red flowers. French windows looked out on the black garden. Millie wanted to sit down, and there were chairs arranged around a breakfast table, but another chair caught her eye—in the corner, next to the broad buffet which held the vase, what decorators call an "accent chair." Dark stained wooden legs and arms, with a bold design on the fabric cushion of the seat and back. It attracted Millie's attention because the design of the fabric was identical to the album art of *My Forgotten Summer*. The same green and yellow, the same rough texture. Even the contours of shadow on one side, resembling a woman's shoulder, were the same. Millie sat on the floor before the chair with her glass of water and touched the rough softness of the fabric and gazed at its colors.

She was in the record store, searching for Artificial Flowers. The shelves were filled with innumerable CDs, marked by white plastic tabs etched with black marker designating letters in the alphabetic filing system as well as the names of prominent bands. Artificial Flowers didn't have their own tab, but even in the "A" section none of their releases could be found.

"Can I help you find something?"

A pretty blonde girl smiled at Millie. Her nametag said Eliza. Millie had been to this record store many times and no one had ever asked if she needed assistance. She wondered if this girl was flirting. It was hard to tell. For a moment they stared at one another. The girl named Eliza brushed her hair behind her ear.

The last time Millie had listened to *My Forgotten Summer* was exactly three years prior, when she had lived with her friend Thomas after graduating from high school. Thomas had *My Forgotten Summer* on vinyl, and they listened to it often, smoking pot and cigarettes on the deck, drinking coffee, talking about video games and music and capitalism, and sometimes making out. Sometimes she would hold the album cover in her hands and stare at the artwork while the music burst from the speakers in jagged ribbons of pain and feeling.

She had been wanting to listen to it again. Was it as good as she remembered? She'd changed so much over the years and she wondered if the album had changed too, or if it would still be just like the deck at Thomas's house and the memory of the smell of pot and deodorant and sunlight and cigarettes.

But all these thoughts crumbled away like dry leaves and cigarette ash. Everything was burned away in the shining desert of Eliza's face. And so Millie forgot what she was looking for. She didn't care anymore. Instead of asking for help, asking if the Artificial Flowers CD could be special-ordered, a lie sprang into her throat and spilled from her lips.

"I'm looking for a job," she said. "Are you hiring?"

Eliza's face brightened, her smile and her eyes widening. Millie felt she had read the situation correctly, and she returned the smile.

"Actually, I think we could use some help," said Eliza. "You'll have to talk to the boss. If you want, I can see if he's available right now?"

While Eliza went to the manager's office, Millie drifted away from the colorful, ceiling-high stacks of CDs and cassette tapes, to the window. She remembered suddenly that the record store was high up, on the 15th floor of a building. Gazing out the narrow window at the adjacent buildings, and at the park and the streets below, her knees buckled with vertigo.

"He's free right now if you want to go see him."

"Yeah. Okay."

They stared at one another in silence. "Do you want to get a drink later?"

Eliza doubled over with laughter, then pushed the hair out of her blushing face. "Yes, definitely."

Millie got her number. It was that easy—like something in a dream. And then she went into the manager's office.

The office strongly resembled the library in the Ross house. The walls were covered by bookshelves filled with literature and philosophy. Seated at a desk was a man with graying black hair and trendy square-frame glasses— Professor Dennis Gray. He smiled and blinked at Millie, and gestured at the chair in front of his desk.

"Please, sit down. So tell me. Do you have any experience in retail?"

"Yes," said Millie. "When I was growing up, my Dad got sick and had to quit his job. I had to start work at the grocery store to help Mom pay the bills. I worked at that job for four years, then when I started college I got a job at the campus cafeteria. But I was raised to work hard and I'm good at figuring out new jobs. Plus I love music, so…"

Dennis smiled. "That's very good," he said. "We're only interested in hiring people with real passion. Do you like punk rock?"

"Yes."

"Good, good. You know, I was just listening to Victimhood. What do you think is their best album?"

MILO'S COMMUTE

His favorite album plays softly as the smell of human hair fills his nostrils, her scalp and her dress filling his lungs. It's not necessary to speak, because everything is held in the tension of the music, in the touch of their hands, in the smell of hair. He doesn't want to speak, or dance, or fuck, or watch television, or drink, or draw. Anchored, transfixed, suspended in that state of lucid grief, like when you wake up in the night to the sound of a train whistle and the black pavement shines with a layer of rainwater glinting in the streetlights, thick black telephone cables draped through dark trees where the moon hides, and the train whistle comes again, and everything is quiet and forgiven, even if terror is there too, she is redeemed and becomes sacred and the earth is empty and real.

Such were the moments that were possible between people who had found something in one another.

The problem was, he didn't have it, he didn't have—what? He didn't have something, something people wanted. They wanted it, and had to find it elsewhere, because he didn't have it. He searched everywhere for it, tried to fake it, or to discover or invent it. As he got older, he became more confident that in fact he did have it, he had it all along, but for some reason no one else could see it. But instead of comforting him, this realization only made things worse. Because if he really did have it, that something that everyone was searching for, then why didn't they want it from him?

Anyway, it wasn't from him, it was with him, because that something isn't real, it's always a dream. Being with her, she was his dream…It didn't even have to be about him, but just about that moment. Wasn't anyone else starved for that moment? He was starved for it, ravenous for it…wasn't she ravenous too?

He felt a wooziness in his legs. The drawings had been rejected, again. They didn't want them. Didn't want *him*…

The breakup had been a revelation for Milo. He was 29 years old. It was now or never. He was going to be an artist. And yet, he still thought about Acacia.

Acacia was a year older than Milo, but her new boyfriend had only just turned 20. His name was Noah. He was a photographer and a skateboarder who dressed, nostalgically and semi-ironically, in an approximation of the style of clothing that was popular when Milo himself was a teenager.

When Acacia initially suggested to Milo that they "open up" their relationship and begin dating other people on the side, Milo was excited. His mind raced through years of missed connections at the farmer's market and the bar, of friends and coworkers who might have been something more had he not already been committed to Acacia…

In practice, however, the year of the "open" relationship was, for Milo, a downward spiral of disappointments. Was it just bad luck, or something worse? He couldn't be sure. In any case, while Milo was getting ignored, rejected, and stood up, and occasionally having sex with women he didn't like which he then regretted painfully the next morning, Acacia was exploring dramatic new heights, and depths, of sexual and romantic experience.

At the very beginning, Milo enjoyed hearing about the men she slept with, who were invariably much older or much younger than he was. Though the intensity and duration of her sex with these other men far exceeded what Milo thought was normal or even safe, it was still titillating to hear about, to experience vicariously. To know that so many men desired Acacia, that she was an object of sexual desire and pleasure for them, gratified and excited Milo, and they often had sex after she finished telling him about her adventures.

But as time went on, and Acacia's exploits continued to mount both in sheer volume and in the eccentricity and licentiousness of the sexual and parasexual practices she engaged in with her partners, and while Milo's slow and painful attempts at courtship with other women continued to prove fruitless, the thrilling novelty of the situation faded and, more and more, Milo sank into a state of dejection and loneliness.

The real turning point came when Acacia came home one morning after having spent the night at a sex party in which a group of men "ran a train" on her, a phrase Milo had never heard before but which apparently meant that several men (in this case, five of them between the ages of 27 and 43) took turns having sex with a woman (in this case, Acacia) one after the other. By the time the last one was finished, the first one was ready to go again.

While Milo lay in bed next to Acacia, listening to the narrative of this encounter in excruciating detail, a dark cloud came over him. He became physically cold. He became deeply and immensely sad. His body became nothing but cold, heavy sadness. And he began to cry.

Three weeks later, they were broken up. Six years of love, suffering, compromise, material and spiritual entanglement, was ended. Milo told her he didn't want to be "open" anymore, that it was causing him pain; Acacia was furious. She already knew he was in pain, and his pain was stifling her, suffocating her; she was a victim of his unhappiness. They fought, she spoke bitterly, but held something back. Milo suspected what it was, and a week later his suspicions were confirmed. She confessed to him that, yes, she was also ready to be monogamous again— just not with Milo. She'd already found someone else.

And so Acacia left. She took her designer kitchenware, the poodle (Toby), and, of course, her trust fund.

The breakup was devastating, but for Milo it was a revelation. He was 29 years old. He was going to turn 30 in the winter. It was now or never. He was going to be an artist. He still thought about Acacia, but he knew there was someone else out there for him, someone else for him to love. And if he succeeded with his art, if he became the kind of person he knew he could be, an artist, then this person, whoever she was, wherever she was, she would recognize him, and she would love him too.

When his tears were dry, Milo rallied himself and made plans. A new chapter in his life was beginning. He was alone, he was free, and the future was open to him. He wasn't old—actually, he was in his prime. This was going to be his decade.

Without the subsidy of Acacia's trust fund (set up by her father, a corporate attorney), it would be impossible for Milo to afford rent anywhere in the city on the meager salary he earned from working at the scented candle emporium. And so he decided to move to the suburbs, to the cheapest place he could possibly find. If he had to sleep on the floor in someone's attic that's what he would do. He wasn't going to waste his hours at the scented candle emporium anymore. He was going to draw.

To Milo's surprise, it was not, however, necessary to sleep on the floor in anyone's attic, or even in their basement. The cheapest place he could find was a comfortable-looking bedroom in a house on a quiet residential street. The cost of utilities was included, and he'd even have access to a washer and dryer and his own private bathroom. What's more, the train station was mere minutes away by foot, making it easy to commute into the city. It was almost too good to be true. He called the number from the online listing immediately and talked to the owner of the house, a pleasant-sounding man named Ray. Milo made arrangements to visit at once.

With rent this low, Milo could survive on his savings alone for a couple of months at least. That would buy him enough time to start making an income on his art. The situation was perfect. It was a stroke of excellent luck, a good omen of things to come.

The train ride to the suburbs was pleasant enough, and took less than an hour. Milo, in high spirits, sketched in his notebook the entire time.

Just as advertised, the house was practically next door to the train station. A tangled, overgrown hedgerow, littered with plastic bags and empty bottles, was all that separated the strip of houses from the tracks. After the train left the station, Milo crossed over the track, then turned down the road that ran parallel to it. Ray's house was the third one down.

It was a two-story craftsman style house, forest green with a cream trim. A family of bearded gnomes with belted tunics and pointed red hats stood proudly before the white begonias in the flower bed. The lawn was tidy and redolent of a fresh mowing. Milo stood on the sidewalk in the late summer light, looking at the house. For the first time that day, he hesitated—not from doubt, but from a sudden pang of self-pity, the kind that comes from knowing one has no choice but to go ahead, to walk down the path, past the gnomes and onto the porch and ring the bell, no matter how pathetic it all was.

Milo pressed the white button next to the door (a classic, electronic two-note bell), and a few moments later the front door opened.

"You must be Milo. I'm Ray. It's nice to meet you, come on in."

Ray held open the storm door as Milo passed through the threshold, smelling the cologne which seemed to perfectly match the man's thick brown mustache, receding hairline, glasses, and blue plaid shirt tucked into white chinos. Blue eyes gleamed through the lenses of his square-frame glasses as he smiled broadly, lips closed tight.

The living room reminded Milo of his grandmother's house. It was dark and the furniture was old and deeply settled into the room. There were white doilies on the wooden end tables, and a stack of National Geographic magazines on the shelf underneath the coffee table. There was a fireplace, a mantle with an antique clock resting on it, and above that a large oil painting of a black schnauzer.

"That's Maxine," said Ray proudly, noticing Milo staring at the portrait. "She died six years, nine months, and eleven days ago today."

"I'm very sorry to hear that," replied Milo.

"She lived a good life, a terrific life," explained Ray reassuringly. "She was well loved. And she is well remembered in this house."

"Yes," said Milo awkwardly.

Ray cleared his throat. "Please, have a seat. Can I get you anything? Water, tea?"

"I'm good, thanks."

They sat down across from one another on a pair of stiff, green velvet sofas. Ray sat with his legs spread apart, his loafers firmly planted on the rug, and his hands on his knees.

"So, tell me about yourself," he said.

Over the course of years Milo had perfected the art of talking about himself, remaining as vague as possible while giving the impression that he had communicated something of substance. He didn't mention anything about Acacia or the breakup, but simply explained he was a full-time artist who needed an affordable place to stay.

At the mention of art, Ray smiled. "I'm no stranger to the art world," he said. "I've commissioned several works of art, like that painting of Maxine."

Milo nodded enthusiastically. "It's a lovely painting," he said.

"You'll be wanting to see the room," said Ray. "Follow me."

He led Milo up the creaky stairs to the second floor landing, where he pointed out the doors to his own bedroom, the bathroom, and linen closet, and then opened the door to the spare bedroom where Milo would be staying.

The room was clean, if somewhat stale. The comforter on the queen-sized bed looked, by Milo's estimate, to be five or possibly six decades old; its dark green color matched the paint on the walls. There was ample space, a tall dresser and closet, and most importantly, a large antique writing desk adjacent to the window.

"May I?" said Milo, gesturing to the desk.

Ray smiled and gestured for him to go ahead. Milo sat down in the wooden chair, which had a welcoming wicker back which groaned appreciatively as he settled into it. Making himself comfortable, he extended his right wrist as if he were about to start drawing. The space and light were nearly ideal. The feeling of pity and apprehension, which had scarcely improved after meeting Ray, now vanished. He was feeling triumphant again.

"It's perfect," he said.

"I'm glad to hear it," replied Ray. "There's just one thing you should know about."

He crossed behind Milo to the window.

"The train comes through right here," he explained, looking out the window past the trees to the track. "It can be quite loud, especially early in the morning."

"I don't mind that at all," said Milo. "I'm used to living in the city. I can handle the noise. Besides, I like trains."

He stood up.

"It's yours if you want it," said Ray.

"Excellent. I can write you a check right now. I'll be back tomorrow with my things."

They shook hands. And that was that.

A muddy wasteland of tall, yellow grass and brown ponds, cut through with dirt trails and electrical lines. In the distance, trucking depots, gas refineries, and gray skies.

Milo didn't mind the commute. In fact, he rather liked it. It gave him time to think. In transit he felt relieved of all responsibility. The train conductor was in charge, and the locomotive was on a fixed track. For the duration of the trip, there was nothing that reasonably could be expected of Milo, and very little that could go wrong. He was simply a passenger, a role not necessarily of passivity but of leisure. In the six weeks since he'd been living at Ray's house he'd made the trip into the city only a handful of times, each time to bring in his portfolio. Each time he'd made a day of it, hitting up a gallery show, treating himself to a drink at a bar, or visiting an old friend (though, truth be told, there weren't many of those still living in the city anymore). Each time the commute was pleasant, relaxing, almost meditative, and this time was no different, even though on this trip he'd be seeing Acacia for the first time since they split up. Yes, he still had feelings for her, but so what? Milo had found someone else, finally. In love and in work, he was ready to be patient, to grow, to build, to discover. The strange wasteland between the suburbs and the city filled him with a sense of desolate peace.

So far, Ray had proven a perfectly fine landlord. Rent was cheap, he gave Milo his privacy, and he even shared meals and coffee with him without asking for any help with the grocery bill. There were only a couple of things that had troubled Milo so far. One was Ray himself. He was an engineer, he said, but he worked from home, in some sort of basement office which Milo had never seen. The door was near the kitchen, and opened on a narrow flight of stairs of unpainted wood, leading to the yellow light of the basement. All Milo had seen were these stairs, and this glow of artificial light. Ray always locked the door behind him when he entered with his mug of coffee to work, disappearing all day until dinner time, and often again late into the night after dinner, only resurfacing for more coffee or to make himself a sandwich in the kitchen.

Milo was bothered, unreasonably and inexplicably, by the existence of the basement office and by the amount of time Ray spent down there. He much would have preferred for Ray to leave the house for work, so that Milo could really have the place to himself. There was nothing in particular that Milo wanted to do aside from just breathing easy, relaxing, and working with the knowledge that he was completely alone. But this was not possible, because as far as Milo could tell, Ray never left the house. Because he worked from home, and groceries were delivered, there was never any reason for him to step outside the confines of the property. He went outside to mow the lawn, tend to the flowerbed, and pace the perimeter of the house, but he never even ventured as far as the sidewalk. Once, when Milo was peering out an upper floor window at Ray while the latter was outside, with the hope that maybe this time Ray would finally leave to go for a stroll or walk to the corner store, he noticed the older gentleman who lived across the street, who at that moment was hosing down the sedan parked in his driveway. Ray was standing in his own, empty, driveway, his hands stuck in his pockets, simply watching his neighbor wash the car. Milo expected the two of them to strike up a conversation, hoping vaguely that Ray would cross the street to chat, and that maybe the two of them would go inside the other's house for a cup of coffee, granting Milo at least a small taste of solitude and, more importantly, proving that Ray was in fact capable of leaving the property. But the two of them did not chat, they did not even exchange any words. When the man across the street, a jowly, balding pensioner wearing slacks and a sweater over a collared shirt, noticed Ray staring at him, he gave a small start and almost dropped his hose. Then, in an indignant huff, he tossed the hose into the grass, bent down on shaky legs to shut off the valve, then stormed inside. While this went on, Ray did not budge, but remained standing erect in the driveway, watching.

Afterward Milo couldn't shake the odd feeling that the whole episode gave him. Clearly, there was bad blood between the two of them, probably a result of some neighborly dispute, perhaps relating to Ray's now-deceased schnauzer Maxine. But for some reason the whole thing gave Milo the creeps. Once or twice, or actually a few times, he thought he noticed other people from the neighborhood staring at the house, or trying to avoid staring at it, as they passed by, and they invariably seemed to pass on the opposite side of the street, as if they didn't want to use the sidewalk on Ray's side. Sometimes Milo could hear Ray's voice from the basement, presumably on video calls with clients or work colleagues (calls which occasionally became, from the sound of it, fairly spirited), but he hadn't seen Ray speak to anyone in person aside from the boy who delivered groceries once a week, and the delivery agent who brought unmarked packages of various sizes to the front porch, which Ray always took directly down to the basement.

Sometimes Milo caught Ray staring out the kitchen window, or at the portrait of Maxine, or, most unsettling of all, standing at the base of the stairs and gazing up blankly in the direction of Milo's room. He was an odd one, that was for sure, but Milo never felt truly disturbed by this behavior, and certainly not threatened, because at all times Ray was perfectly friendly. And if Milo caught him in one of his thousand-yard stares, Ray would, after a moment, blink and remember himself, and strike up a cordial and non-intrusive conversation about Milo's art or some other topic. He was simply a strange and reclusive person, which was why his neighbors tended to avoid him. But for an artist seeking peace and quiet, he was (almost) an ideal roommate.

But there was one other thing. The sound…

The train groaned to a stop as it reached a station at the edge of the yellow wasteland. The landscape had changed to highway overpasses, old brick warehouses, and shopping centers. A pretty girl got on the train and sat within view of Milo's seat. He stared idly at the side of her head, her black hair which in the gray light of the morning was the perfect shade of black, and he thought about drawing her just like this, sitting on the train and staring at her phone.

The train began to move. The sound, what was it? The sound that Milo heard in his room at night—the faint, slow, mechanical clacking and grinding. It was not the radiator or the groaning of pipes. It was too distinct, too close. It didn't always wake Milo up, but when it did, the sound filled him with instant, unaccountable dread. It sounded like a machine had been switched on inside his room. The first few times, Milo simply shut his eyes, ignored the sound, and went back to sleep. But on subsequent nights it became too much to bear, his mind too oppressed by nightmarish suggestions of what might be producing it, fantasies which, as they became more vivid and bizarre, seemed to cause the sound itself to become louder, closer, more insistent, and more grotesque. Finally one night Milo threw off the blankets, switched on the lights, and searched his room for the clockwork thing, the wind-up doll which had been unleashed to crawl around his floor, or whatever it was. But there was nothing. And as soon as he turned on the lights, the sound ceased completely, and would not return for the rest of the night. Was it all in his imagination, somehow? The next morning over breakfast, he found the courage to finally broach the matter with Ray.

"It's the train," said Ray happily as, with a pair of shining metal tongs, he served hot bacon from a platter, nestling the strips of meat next to the pancakes on Milo's plate. "Freight trains use the track late at night sometimes."

The freight train often did wake Milo up—its slow, heavy trundling, the blast of its whistle. But these sounds never disturbed Milo. On the contrary, he found them comforting, rustic, almost mystical. In any case, it was easy to distinguish the resonant rumbling of the freight train from outside the window, with the metallic clacking which was clearly coming from inside, or very nearby, Milo's room.

"I don't think so…" Milo protested as Ray settled in across from him at the table and began to butter his steaming pancakes. "I know the sound of the train. It's not like that at all…"

"I don't mean to argue, but I know a thing or two about trains," said Ray with a sharp twinkle in his eye as he dispensed maple syrup over his flapjacks. "They play tricks on you."

Milo didn't know how to press the issue, so he left it at that, and tucked into his breakfast. The sound during subsequent nights didn't go away, but by searching his room thoroughly he contented himself that it must be coming from inside the walls, that it was indeed merely the murmuring and ticking of pipes, or some other house noise, the breathing and settling of wood, the sighing and snoring of walls and floors and stairs after a long day of supporting human habitation. It didn't sound like any of this, but there was no other explanation. And so Milo forced himself to be satisfied.

Milo looked at his sketch—the head of black hair, the shoulders, the hands holding the phone, the smokestacks and the lattice of power lines and phone cables visible in the window behind her. These days he did almost nothing but draw. He had brought in his old architect lamp and set it up on the desk in his new bedroom. In the mornings and early afternoon he drank coffee and worked with ink, in the evenings he drank whiskey and sketched with pencil and charcoal. At twilight he would often go for walks alongside the train tracks, kicking through the tall grass and the old beer cans and soda bottles until it became dark. Sometimes Ray made dinner, sometimes the two of them made sandwiches and ate separately. At night Milo watched old movies on his laptop computer and tried to talk to women on a dating app on his phone.

He was lonely, there was no question of that, and at first the dating app had only made it worse. Women would stop talking to him after only exchanging a few messages, or else they would be too eager and he would be the one to lose interest. He hated the mechanical nature of it. Browsing through the profiles of women felt too much like shopping. He didn't like the way he had to present himself, to summarize his entire existence in a handful of images and phrases, and he didn't like the way it habituated him to perceiving women as objects in a catalog. It was a depressing enterprise, a slog, sifting through all those women, getting rejected from people he was only barely attracted to in the first place. But just as he was beginning to lose hope, he found Kyra.

It was just the night before. Milo was feeling faintly ill at the prospect of seeing Acacia again, and he'd started drinking earlier than usual. Then he got the notification on his phone—a new match on the dating app. Kyra, Kyra, Kyra…

He started with a joke, she replied, and they ended up talking for close to three hours. She was an artist. She was beautiful. Her name was Kyra.

Suddenly, metal screeched and hissed as the train made an unexpected stop somewhere between stations. Outside the window, a grassy slope covered with decades of trash, an abandoned chain-link fence sagging under the weight of brown vines and plastic debris. After a few minutes, a conductor appeared in the car and explained that the train had hit something, a living thing. Protocol dictated that the police had to be called to determine whether or not it was a human being.

Milo's anonymous model, the girl with the black hair, made a phone call.

"Hey, sorry, I might be late. The train is held up. Yeah, we hit someone…I know, right? It's probably just some homeless person. So fucking annoying."

"We appreciate you coming in, we really do. But this simply isn't what we're looking for."

Milo had heard variations of this polite rejection already at the magazines, book publishers, advertising firms, and art galleries where he'd brought in his portfolio on his previous commutes to the city. But this time would be different. Before, he'd been too eager, he'd been showing off old work from the past few years, from his time with Acacia. Since splitting up and dedicating himself to art, everything had changed. His technique improved rapidly with hours of daily practice, and his new life, as dreary as it often felt, was also marked by fresh perspective, a sense of freedom, of possibility. He'd finished several smaller charcoal pieces now that he was quite proud of, and just in the past week he had completed an ink drawing that was, without exaggeration, the best thing he'd ever produced. Bold, masterful lines, subtle use of color, a penetrating and totally original insight into the subject, hinting diagonally at social critique in a way that was edgy, surprising, but still well within the parameters of correct opinion—Milo himself was stunned by his own work, and he was sure it could not fail to impress even the most jaded gallery owner. His social media profiles so far had failed to gain traction, but with the recent breakthrough in his work he was confident he'd begin to get some attention. Even without gallery representation, he could promote himself online. There was every reason to be optimistic. This was the beginning.

"We appreciate you coming in, we really do, but…"

She had studied the drawings for several minutes, leafing through the portfolio on her desk, occasionally humming appreciatively. At the end, she'd opened the separate manila folder containing the *pièce de résistance*, the new ink drawing. But as she examined it, Milo couldn't help but feel that the pained look on her face was not one of careful appreciation, but something bordering on pity. She idly touched her neck as she searched for the best words, and then, finally meeting Milo's eyes, she said:

"This isn't what we're looking for."

It wasn't easy to get a meeting, however brief, with a gallery owner, even at a small gallery like this. Milo didn't like sending in a digital portfolio. He wanted to meet in person, he wanted them to see the work in person, to hold it, touch it. He wanted to make an impression. As he gathered up his work, thanked her for her time, and saw himself out of her office, he certainly felt like he'd made an impression, but of the worst possible kind. He wanted to feel defiant, but in the moment found this impossible. He strode out of the gallery with his head down, ignoring the attendant at the front desk who wished him a nice day.

It shouldn't matter so much. It was just one gallery. But something about the way she'd looked at the work, something about the way she'd squinted at it, curling her lips inward, tempted to say certain things but deciding against it…

Milo tried to dispel the humiliation with a deep sigh as he walked toward the subway station. It was just one gallery. He couldn't think about it anymore now. It was almost 11, and he had to get to his next appointment.

Given the season, the fountain should have been filled with water, but instead it was shut off. The inside of the concrete pool was covered with pink and green graffiti.

Kids on skateboards sailed up and down its sides, doing tricks and crashing, while their friends sat on the lip of the pool drinking energy drinks and smoking cigarettes.

"Milo, oh my God!"

Acacia was wearing a mauve floral sundress, black beret, and black boots. In one hand she held a plastic cup of iced coffee, in the other hand, the leash which led to the collar of a large, brown poodle. A large tote bag, emblazoned with the insignia of a popular local book store, hung heavily over one shoulder. With her hands full and unable to hug Milo properly, she extended both arms, smiling and opening herself, and allowed him to embrace her.

"You look great. How have you been?"

"I'm doing really well, actually. And you look fantastic as always."

They sat on a bench. The poodle, Toby, eagerly greeted Milo by licking his hands.

"Toby missed you," said Acacia sweetly. "I've missed you, too. How's the art life?"

"Better than ever. I just met with a gallery owner this morning…"

"Oh, Milo! That's wonderful! Are they interested?"

"Who knows? It's all very complicated. But it's just one gallery. I've made a breakthrough with my work. It happened suddenly. Splitting up was hard, but somehow it woke me up. It was like for years I'd been half-asleep. It was like—"

"Can I have an energy drink?"

There was a boy or young man, dressed like one of the skaters, standing nervously behind Acacia. He had his hands folded nervously in front of him.

Acacia groaned and began digging through her tote bag, which jangled with loose metal and plastic.

"Here," she said, handing him a cylindrical black can and brushing the hair out of her face. "Wait, don't run off. This is Milo, who I've told you about. Toby's dad. Milo, this is Colby."

Colby smiled awkwardly, revealing a mouth full of braces. "Nice to meet you," he said.

Quite lost, Milo could only nod vaguely. Colby turned around then and walked back to the empty fountain, where he began talking with another young man, similarly dressed, who Milo suddenly recognized as Acacia's boyfriend Noah.

"Aren't they so cute?" said Acacia, gazing at the pair and clasping her hands.

"Are you…"

"I know what you're thinking—it must be a handful, dating them both. But they don't get jealous of each other! When Noah told me he was bisexual, I just knew we had to get another boy in the bedroom. So I found Colby. He had just turned 18. Yes, he's still in high school, going to start his senior year this fall, but his parents were fine with him moving in with us. They're very progressive. Especially when I offered to pay for Colby's orthodontics. Anyway, it's been perfect. Two is enough, I don't think I could handle three—but who knows? Anyway, how about your love life? Are you seeing anyone?"

Milo was focused on petting Toby, digging his fingers into his rough, curly hair, scratching him behind the ears and on the shoulders. "Yes," he said, without meeting Acacia's eyes. "Yes, I've met someone…"

"Oh, Milo, I'm so glad to hear that. I've been worried about you…Tell me about her?"

"Her name's Kyra. She's an artist."

"How long have you been seeing her?"

"Not very long…But I think there's something there."

"Oh, Milo. I'm so happy for you."

She was being earnest, painfully earnest. The tone of her voice told Milo everything: that it was over, permanently finished. There was no hope of their ever getting back together. Milo, for Acacia, was no longer an object of desire, or love, but of pity. He was like a Caribbean or African orphan child on a television advertisement for some Christian charity: dehumanized, rendered as an animal for the appreciation of rich Western women. Milo rubbed Toby even more vigorously.

"I should be going," he said abruptly. "I'm meeting Derrick."

They embraced. This time Acacia set her iced coffee on the ground first so she could put at least one arm around Milo.

"Alright boys, time to go," she called to Noah and Colby. "Say goodbye to your friends."

Milo arrived at the restaurant early and ordered a shot of tequila and a bottle of cheap Mexican lager. He took the shot, tried and failed to suck juice from the dry lime wedge the waitress had given him, and then took a long drink of the beer. He wanted to finish it before Derrick arrived, to hide the fact that he'd already begun drinking.

Derrick was the last of Milo's close friends who still lived in the city, and now he too was moving away. He'd taken a teaching job, part-time at a liberal arts college in the middle of nowhere. He was a conceptual artist, or he had been, but now he was giving it up permanently to be a writer instead. Practically every artist Milo once knew in the city had either left to pursue an art career in another town or else abandoned their dreams entirely.

Condensation pooled on the checkered vinyl tablecloth. Milo dragged a finger through it absently. On his way from the park to the restaurant he had texted Kyra, and since then he'd been checking his phone over and over to see if she'd replied. He resisted the urge to do so again, and instead stared listlessly at the muted television broadcast of a soccer match while he finished his beer.

Derrick wore small circular glasses and odd t-shirts salvaged from thrift stores. His arms were covered in black tattoos of electronic circuitry mixed with lines of Spanish poetry. He moved and spoke very precisely, though with frequent hesitations and false starts, aborting imprudent trains of thought or action to pause, twist his mouth, touch his left canine tooth with the tip of his index finger as he reconsidered, either going in a different direction or deciding to do or say nothing at all. He arrived a few minutes late, sidling past a waitress and easing himself into the booth across from Milo, whose fresh beer had just arrived at the table. He had on a white t-shirt bearing the logo of a popular brand of anti-depressant prescription drug tucked into faded blue jeans, and a burgundy knitted skullcap.

"It's been too long. How are the suburbs treating you?"

"There's nothing to do. It's perfect. I'm drawing all day."

The waitress came around. They ordered tacos and Milo insisted on tequila. Derrick listened attentively while Milo told him about his embarrassment at the gallery, and about his meeting with Acacia. The tequila arrived, along with more useless lime wedges, and they drank it.

"Well," said Derrick. "Are you going to show me the work?"

Milo handed him the manila folders from his messenger bag and studied Derrick's expression as he leafed through the drawings. When he was done, he squinted off at a corner of the ceiling and touched his canine tooth while he gathered his thoughts. The waitress brought plates of tacos, and Milo scrambled to gather up his drawings and move them out of the way so she could put them down.

"I shouldn't have told you about the woman at the gallery," Milo lamented as he put the drawings back in his messenger bag. "I should have had you look at the work first, without any preconceptions…"

"Everything, or rather, I should say, all art is bound up with preconceptions," replied Derrick. "There's no way around it." He began eating his tacos, salsa and sour cream dripping down his fingers.

"How are your finances?" asked Derrick as they walked from the restaurant to the gallery, which was a couple of blocks away.

"Fine," replied Milo. Then, after a pause: "No, not fine. I have some savings, still, but I need to be making money. I've tried a variety of things, but I haven't made a fucking penny from art."

Derrick hummed. He seemed to be considering something, which for the time he held back.

"It's hard," he said. "It's becoming impossible to be an artist in this city anymore. It's just too expensive. At least you're saving money by living in the suburbs."

Milo was drunk. He'd had three tequilas and three beers at the restaurant, and only eaten half of his food.

"Do you think it's impossible?" he said. "For me. Do you think…I'm impossible? You saw my work, what I'm trying to do right now. Do you think it's impossible?"

"Here we are," said Derrick, gesturing to the gallery doors.

It was the opening day of a traveling exhibition of paintings by René Magritte.

"I worked my ass off for that woman," said Milo as they wandered from one painting to the next, moving past yuppies and college students taking pictures on their phones. "She could have paid for our apartment, our whole lifestyle, with her trust fund. She could have supported us both so that I could have dedicated myself to drawing. Instead I worked, for years, when I could have dedicated those years to my art, to my life. And then when she gets tired of me, she throws me out. She could have married me. She could have married a great artist. It's not her fault. I should have left a long time ago…"

They arrived at the centerpiece in the main room of the gallery, one of Magritte's most famous works: *Time Transfixed.* An empty fireplace, with a clock and two bare candles on its mantle in front of a mirror; from the middle of the cold fireplace, a black locomotive bursts into existence, steam jetting from its chimney, racing into the empty room.

"You still never told me what you think about my drawings."

Derrick gave a controlled sigh, like a piece of machinery emitting a burst of steam. "The truth is I think you're still too close to everything. You're pandering to the establishment—or, rather, to some idea of what you think the establishment wants. Your technique is there, but the vision is too straight and narrow. You have to find some darkness. You have to confront the obscene, you have to go off the rails…Have you been to this new gallery, Garrote Wire? Now that's the cutting edge. They're really trying to cultivate something new there, to make art dangerous again. You should check it out, you might get inspired. Milo, are you listening?"

Milo was not listening. He was transfixed by *Time Transfixed.* He had always been repulsed by this painting without knowing why, but now, seeing it in person for the first time he understood. It was smug. It was the preening of a delusional genius, executed with the lazy mastery of a grade-A student, playing at insanity but devoid of myth, devoid of real suffering.

"You know what really pisses me off, more than anything? It's not the gallery owners. It's not Acacia. It's the fact that *I'm better than Magritte.*"

"Milo, keep your voice down."

"It's true! I *am* better than him. Do you disagree?"

An old woman touched her wrinkled wattle neck, staring with distress at Milo before turning and moving away from the painting. A trio of thin, attractive undergraduates dressed in black seemed to be suppressing giggles, suddenly looking away from the painting and becoming interested in their phones. Derrick was still figuring out what to say next.

"He's mediocre," said Milo, lowering his voice but still seething. "He was just in the right place at the right time…"

"*But that's all there is,*" hissed Derrick, stepping closer and whispering in Milo's ear as if this were sensitive but urgent information. "There is no universal criterion for art. All we have are places and times. It's not enough for you to be better than Magritte in some abstract sense. You have to be better than *your time*, better than *your place*."

Derrick looked over his shoulder, then gently grabbed Milo's arm. "Come on," he said. "Let's get out of here."

Rays of afternoon sun, slanting down side streets, blazed on the glass towers. Milo's limbs glowed with a drunken, euphoric self-pity.

"I'm going to text you a link," said Derrick.

They were walking down the sidewalk, toward the subway station.

"A link to what?"

"A way to make money."

"From art?"

"From drawing."

They paused at the entrance to the subway, the dirty stairs leading to tunnels, to rats, bums, the smell of piss and sweat, to the specter of suicide which loomed on the edge of every track.

"A friend of mine makes his entire income this way," said Derrick. "It's nothing to be ashamed of. It's money. Look into it, okay?"

"Sure," said Milo. He was gazing at the sidewalk, the cement discolored with unknown accumulations of black and gray stains. "Thank you…I'm sorry…"

"Don't apologize. You're going to be alright."

They embraced with the unspoken sense that they might not see one another again for years, if ever.

Time transfixed. That was indeed how it felt to be on a train. Perhaps that's what Magritte was getting at. Maybe Milo had been too harsh…

He got off the subway and onto the commuter rail which would take him back to the suburbs, back to Ray's house. Messages came through on his phone: one from Derrick, one from Kyra.

His whole being surged to see Kyra's name appear on his phone, but he didn't want to appear desperate by texting her back too quickly. And anyway, the unopened message in his inbox was like a little present, a treat he could save for later when he got home and poured himself a drink.

Milo opened the message from Derrick. It was a link, as promised, and as Milo opened it and watched the web page load on his phone's internet browser, he at first thought Derrick had played a joke on him, and he laughed out loud. But then, recalling the seriousness with which Derrick had urged him to consider it, he read on.

The website was an online marketplace for pornographic art. Specifically, it was for selling drawings which catered to niche fetishists who struggled to find expression of their fantasies elsewhere, even amid the internet's vast, free libraries of obscene materials. Clients commissioned works from artists, and the website took a small fee. According to the page detailing the terms for artists, the average price for a commissioned work was considerable.

After looking at these numbers, and remembering Derrick's words—that a friend of his maintained his entire income from this kind of work—Milo chuckled. The train had emerged from the industrial park into the blond wasteland, shining in the late afternoon sun. Work was work, and hadn't Milo's dream been to make money from drawing? His savings would be entirely depleted soon if he didn't do something, and the mere thought of returning to the candle store put the bitter taste of geranium-scented wax in his mouth. So, why not?

Ray greeted Milo wearing an oven mitt on one hand and an apron covered in blue flowers. He was roasting a couple of Cornish hens (his mother's recipe) along with some potatoes. There was to be a salad, also, and wine, all to congratulate Milo on his meeting with the gallery owner.

While Milo was getting washed up before dinner, he tried to remember having mentioned anything to Ray about his trip into the city and his interview with the gallery, but he came up blank. It must have happened offhand at some point in the past week, over breakfast. It was a nice gesture, and Milo was hungry, but there was a lot on his mind and he didn't quite feel like he had the energy to entertain Ray, who would be expecting a lively conversation over dinner, possibly even with dessert afterward, maybe even the dreaded invitation to play cards. To muster the courage for the evening, Milo poured himself a bourbon and opened the message from Kyra:

hey :) hows ur day goin

Milo stared and stared at the message, and then held the corner of his phone against his forehead, shut his eyes, and exhaled. Everything was going to be okay.

Though the meat was slightly dry, the chicken had a gorgeous brown skin, and the wedges of potato, roasted in the oven alongside the birds, were also nice and crispy. Milo drank a lot of wine.

"So, tell me," said Ray once they'd settled down at the table. "How did it go?"

He was smiling in his particular way, friendly but just slightly unsettling, his mouth turned up just barely beneath his bushy mustache, and his bright grayish-blue eyes gleaming like jewels. He had a fork in one hand and a knife in the other, holding them poised over his plate while he waited for Milo to begin his story.

Milo had already cut into his food. He washed down a bite of chicken with a swallow of red wine. "It went well," he said, chewing and nodding, looking down at his plate and avoiding Ray's invasive glare. "Really well."

"Well that's just terrific. Absolutely terrific."

Milo ate a cherry tomato. "Yep," he said. "Things are looking good. And I might have some work coming in, commissions for drawings…"

"Terrific. You know, I've commissioned several works of art, like the painting of Maxine in the living room…"

"Yes, you've mentioned that."

"That reminds me," said Ray somberly, wiping his mustache with a cloth napkin and clearing his throat. "There's a very special day coming up next month. A day we take very seriously in this house. An anniversary."

"Oh?"

"Yes. The anniversary of…Maxine's accident."

"I see."

Ray removed his glasses and covered his face with steepled hands. Milo kept chewing, but tried to do so as noiselessly as possible out of respect.

Clearing his throat again, Ray blinked and put his glasses back on. "You'll have to forgive me," he said. "It's a very emotional time, the whole month leading up to that day. You'd think the pain would fade, but no. Each year it only gets worse."

"Yes, I understand," said Milo sympathetically.

"Anyway, that's all I wanted, was to warn you. If I seem to lose the swing in my step, if old Ray's not as chipper as usual, don't go thinking its because you've done anything wrong. It's just that time of year."

On account of the dinner, and Ray having brought up the painful memory of his dog's untimely death, Milo allowed himself to be pressed into a round of gin rummy. They played in the living room, beneath the silent gaze of Maxine's dark portrait. Declining Ray's offer of coffee, Milo poured himself some bourbon to accompany the dish of vanilla ice cream that was more or less forced upon him. Milo drank and texted Kyra, but Ray was so pleased with himself—dinner had gone well, and it was the first time he'd successfully cajoled Milo into cards—that he didn't seem bothered in the slightest by Milo's preoccupation. Milo even stayed for another round of gin rummy and another scoop of ice cream while he went back and forth with Kyra about their favorite films. He apologized for being on his phone and told Ray he was texting a girl, which pleased Ray considerably. When it was time for Milo to turn in, Ray gave him a smile, seized his shoulder, and squeezed slightly too hard.

"I just knew this would be terrific. You, me. Like a couple of old pals."

They were standing at the base of the stairs. It was impossible to avoid Ray's eyes, his grin. Milo became suddenly conscious that his own face was possibly betraying the chilling unease, bordering on fear, with which he occasionally regarded his landlord, and so he turned his grimace into a yawn, followed by his best effort at a smile.

"Yes," said Milo ambiguously. "Thanks again for dinner."

He sidestepped Ray and began ascending the stairs.

"I'll be working late," said Ray suddenly. Milo paused midway up the stairs but didn't turn around.

"Downstairs," Ray continued. His tone had turned suddenly dark, suddenly ghastly. "In the basement."

"Alright, then. Goodnight."

At the second floor landing, Milo glanced behind him. Ray was still frozen in the half-light at the base of the stairs. Milo closed and locked his bedroom door, poured himself another bourbon from the bottle he'd been carrying around, and got comfortable in his bed to text Kyra some more until he fell asleep.

That night Milo was awakened, as he often was, by the heavy blast of the freight train whistle. He opened his eyes to the darkness of his bedroom, illuminated softly by the glowing window, white stars and yellow street lamps mixing the black night into faint blue. The whistle came again, a sustained note followed by two short blasts, and then the heavy, slow rolling of the mighty wheels on the tracks.

It must have been 2 or 3 in the morning, but it didn't matter whose sleep was disturbed. This mystic passage must be proclaimed.

But then, another sound, *the* other sound: the dreaded clacking, ticking, grinding. Not from the freight train, as Ray had dismissively claimed. There was no question. It was coming from inside the room, and it was louder and more distinct now than ever before.

Milo rolled over so that he was lying on his back. That's when he saw the light.

A tiny sapphire pinprick glowed dimly from the wall at the foot of the bed. It was about two-thirds of the way toward the ceiling and a foot away from the corner of the other wall. And it was moving.

The tinny clicking sound had slowed, but now it matched the pace of this eerie blue light, which was slowly creeping out from the wall, growing bigger, brighter, closer. But then, as if sensing Milo's gaze, the light withdrew. As Milo leaned over to switch on his bedside lamp, there was a flourish of clicks as the blue pinprick diminished. By the time Milo had turned on the lamp, the blue light and the sound both had vanished without a trace. Milo stood on top of his bed, examining the exact spot in the wall while he listened to the trundling of the freight train outside. The wall was just as bare as it always had been, offering no explanation for the sapphire light or the sound.

Milo climbed into bed and cracked open a book he'd checked out from the library, *How To Make It As An Artist*, and read a few dismal pages until he was able to fall back asleep.

The next day Milo bought a flashlight. He knew asking Ray about the mysterious sights and sounds in the bedroom was useless. He also knew he was under a degree of mental strain, and that he'd been drinking too much. In devoting himself so energetically and single-mindedly to only two pursuits—art, primarily, but also finding a girlfriend—he'd neglected both his physical and mental well-being. Though he'd found a certain spiritual equilibrium after the breakup, this was founded on an optimism and forward momentum which it turned out was quite fragile, easily shaken by setbacks which were, though undoubtedly embarrassing, relatively minor when considered soberly. Excess of alcohol, lack of exercise, sexual frustration—all these factors undermined one's psychic cohesion. Nocturnal hallucinations in themselves were nothing to be alarmed about; they could merely be a manifestation of this state of imbalance, a warning sign of wear and tear on the nervous system. Psychological indigestion, essentially.

The flashlight, then, was more for Milo's peace of mind than anything else. If the clacking sound and the pinprick of sapphire light returned, and the flashlight were underneath his pillow, he could reach for it slowly, pretending to still be asleep. And then, pointing it at the blue light, he could turn it on and catch whatever was there, whatever was creeping into his room at night. Or, rather, he wouldn't catch anything at all, because probably there was nothing to catch. But this stratagem could prove once and for all this fact, and then even if Milo kept hearing the sound, he could rest easy knowing it was indeed all in his mind. He imagined moving back into the city, getting an apartment with a girl, maybe Kyra, settling down again, making money from art, drawing all day, cooking meals together with his beloved, making love, sleeping with limbs entangled. A life of peace, but a peace that was alive with the fire of dreams and good sex. An artist's life, a fearless life, in which it would not be necessary to sleep with a flashlight beneath one's pillow. That day would come. But for now, Milo needed the flashlight.

Instinctively, he concealed the purchase of the flashlight from Ray. Milo went for a morning stroll, stopped by the hardware store, bought the small battery-powered flashlight with a pack of batteries, disposed of the packaging, and shoved these things in his pockets. Ray was at work in the basement when Milo returned from his walk, but he hadn't wanted to take any chances. In his bedroom he put batteries in the flashlight, tested it, then placed it under the pillow.

What weighed on Milo's mind perhaps more than anything else, and was doubtless contributing to his brittle nerves, was the question of money. If this could be resolved, he could relax, return to art, redouble his efforts. Money was time, money was space, it was rent and food. Money was, unfortunately, the foundation of art, just as it was the foundation of everything else. And what Milo needed was sturdier foundations. After his trip to the hardware store, he made an account on the erotic commission website and uploaded some sketches to show off his talent, and then settled into his daily drawing routine. After dinner that evening, he logged in to check his account.

To Milo's delight, there was already a message in his inbox. Someone apparently liked his style, and had messaged him with a description of a bizarre albeit not excessively unwholesome sexual scene, to be executed in black-and-white for a modest fee. Milo, already a couple of drinks in, did not hesitate to reply with an enthusiastic *yes*.

Milo grew a beard.

Acacia had hated him with a beard, so when they first started dating he shaved it off. Milo hated shaving, but he had been so accustomed to doing it for her that for weeks since the breakup he'd failed to consider he now had a choice in the matter. And so he grew a beard and took up smoking, just a few cigarettes a day, something else he'd avoided for years because of Acacia but which now, he realized, he was free to enjoy again.

Milo found a lawn chair in Ray's garage and took to sunning in the backyard, shirtless, with his sketchbook or a novel, a glass of iced bourbon lemonade, sometimes a cigarette, soaking in the last days of heat before the weather changed and the leaves lost their bittersweet green.

The combination of Ray's cooking and the alcohol had resulted in Milo gaining a bit of weight. He'd put on something of a writerly paunch, but it was nothing to worry about. There'd be plenty of time to get healthy again later, once his affairs were in order.

Kyra had been busy. Or, rather, not busy, but sick—she'd come down with some savage strain of summer flu which wiped her out for a solid week. No sooner had she recovered then she was on an airplane to visit her parents who lived out of state, plans which had been made months ago. She'd been hoping to see Milo before the trip, they'd made plans to meet for coffee and go to a gallery afterward, but she'd had to cancel as a result of her illness, and now she was traveling. She promised him earnestly that they'd meet as soon as she returned to the city. For now, Milo had to be patient.

Dinner and gin rummy with Ray had become a regular occurrence—twice, sometimes thrice weekly. Milo didn't just do this to be polite. With the anniversary of his beloved dog's death approaching, Ray's behavior, already odd, had become increasingly erratic. Milo frequently caught him dusting the living room, vacuuming the floors, or cleaning the kitchen with feverish alacrity, while tears streamed down his cheeks and he whistled some abnormal tune, like he was desperately but unsuccessfully trying to wrench himself out from a fit of violent despair. Even worse, Milo had been awoken in the night on two separate occasions by the ghastly air of Ray moaning Maxine's name. Ray clearly needed a distraction, and anyway Milo was starting to enjoy playing gin.

As for Milo's art, he was drawing more and more but liking the results less and less. Derrick's words, and the disappointed expression on the face of the gallery owner, haunted his work. Sketches were abandoned halfway through, torn out of his sketchbook to be crumpled and thrown in the trash. He wanted to find some new starting point, some fresh idea, some twist of darkness like Derrick had suggested, but the harder Milo searched for it the more elusive it seemed.

Meanwhile, the commissions kept rolling in, and increasingly Milo found himself devoting his hours to making fetish art for money instead of focusing on his "real" work. Over the past few weeks, one client in particular slowly came to monopolize Milo's attention, for the simple reason that he paid almost double what anyone else offered, and he was always ready with another commission as soon as Milo finished a piece. The problem was the nature of the drawings demanded by this particular client. At first Milo had thought it was funny, but the more drawings he completed the more this layer of humor wore thin, until what was left was discomfort, chills, nausea. He had to drink while he worked on these pieces, and couldn't stand to look at the finished product. The money, though, was just too good to pass up. After only a few weeks he'd assembled a small portfolio of these freakish images, these drawings for a very special client: drawings of anthropomorphized train engines, engaged in grotesque and violent sexual acts.

Milo was making money, finally. He was working, but his real work had fallen off. When he sat down to draw, he found his mind filled with the disgusting images from his commissioned fetish art. These erotic nightmares colonized his imagination, and occasionally appeared in his actual dreams when he wasn't too drunk to have any. It was one such night when, writhing and turning in the throes of these twisted visions, Milo abruptly awoke, thirsty and covered in sweat. He had just turned over on his side, throwing the damp sheet off of his hot skin, when he heard it: the clacking sound.

So far, since hiding the flashlight beneath his pillow, the sound had not returned, or else he'd slept through it each time. But now there it was, and Milo was awake, and ready. The unwholesome shroud of the nightmare still clung to him even as the cool air chilled his flesh, and he was filled with dread. But this was his chance. Pretending still to be asleep, Milo turned again so that now he was facing the wall with a better angle of the corner. Opening his eyes halfway, he saw the pinpoint of blue light, creeping out from the wall with the steady mechanical clacking noise. He slid a hand underneath the pillow.

He had to be quick. He felt for the switch on the side of the flashlight, readied his thumb against it. Pretending to toss again in his sleep, he turned onto his back, withdrawing his hand and aiming the flashlight at the sapphire dot in the corner of the wall. Milo breathed in, held it, steadied his hand, and then with his eyes fixed on the spot, determined to glimpse even for a split second whatever it was, if it was anything, before it vanished, he switched on the flashlight.

Milo opened his mouth, but the scream was frozen in his throat.

The model train, now no longer creeping, suddenly blasted its piercing whistle as it roared into the room, its blue headlight shining. It was on a track built along the side of the wall, a few feet down from the ceiling. The engine came out from a tunnel in the far wall, pulling car after car behind it onto the track.

Milo leaped out of bed and switched on the light, half-expecting the demonic train to vanish back into the hell from whence it came. But no, it was there, it was real, somehow, impossibly. The tunnel and the track, which Milo was utterly confident were not there when he'd gone to sleep that night, had never been there in all his weeks in the room, were as real as anything. Milo found his voice again, the scream unstuck in his throat and came pouring out.

The train was coming for him. Screaming, Milo cowered, as if fearing the ridiculous toy would fly off its tracks and attack him like a black mechanical dragon, and he stumbled backward off the bed, tripping over his desk chair and falling on his ass. Panting, hyperventilating, he watched from the floor as the repulsive thing snaked along the walls and finally exited through another tunnel above his desk.

"Milo?" it was Ray's voice, calling from downstairs. "Milo, is everything alright?"

Milo bounded out of his bedroom, naked except for his boxers, in time to see the model train chugging along the wall in the upstairs hallway, along another track which he was positive had not been there before. Ray must have been working late. He was standing now at the bottom of the stairs, fully dressed, holding a cup of hot tea. Milo regarded his landlord with a dawning, furious abhorrence.

"What's happened?" repeated Ray. "Did you have a bad dream?"

Milo descended the stairs slowly, still gripping the flashlight like a weapon in his sweaty palm. It occurred to him that if he needed to fight, he would probably be best off using it as a projectile, and in that instant he imagined himself as a naked paleolithic man, terrified in the face of an unknown enemy, armed with only his claws and teeth and whatever he could pick up and throw. He almost laughed out loud.

"What the hell was that…that *train* in my room?" he finally said.

Ray frowned. "You mean *my* train?"

"Yes, *your* train!" barked Milo. "How the hell did it get in my room?"

"I warned you about it when you first moved in…"

"No, no, *no*," shouted Milo. He was paused two-thirds of the way down the stairs, looming over Ray, unblinking, ready for anything. "You warned me about the *freight train*, about the noise. The model train wasn't there before. There's a hole in the wall, tracks coming in and circling around. How did it get there? It wasn't there last night."

Ray slurped his steaming hot tea with a look of fatherly concern. The model train engine whistled from some corner of the house as it proceeded with its grotesque nocturnal peregrinations.

"Alright then," said Milo. "I'm leaving here. Tomorrow…"

Ray's jaw dropped open. He looked so hurt that even given the circumstances Milo felt a twinge of guilt.

"But we were getting along so well," he sputtered. "Things have been so terrific. Oh, you can't leave me now. Not this month, of all months…I know what it is. The rent is too high, is that it? I'll tell you what. I'll knock it down by $100. No, make that $200. I know what it's like to be an artist. I'm no stranger to the art world. I know how difficult it can be, and—"

"Okay, okay, listen, let's discuss it in the morning, okay?" Milo cut in. "I have to sleep."

Milo staggered back upstairs, shut out the lights, and crawled into bed, but he couldn't sleep. Had the tracks been there all along, and somehow he'd missed them? Or had Ray come in and silently constructed it all while he slept? This didn't seem possible, considering that tunnels had been cut through the walls. Maybe the tunnels had already been there, and covered by a framed painting, a clock, something like that, which recently had been taken down. Perhaps Milo's state of distraction and exertion and had led him to overlook these things. He'd heard the sound, seen the headlight in the darkness, why had he never seen the tracks, the tunnels, the train? Was he losing his mind?

The freight train whistle resounded in the night, and it was like the presence and weight of the world. Milo found comfort in it, and after a while he managed to drift to sleep.

Had Ray slept at all? He had changed clothes, at least, but he was awake when Milo staggered downstairs soon after dawn. Ray was there, in the kitchen, brewing coffee and whisking eggs. The model train came chugging through a tunnel in the wall into the kitchen, sailing along the track over the stove and the countertops. The morning sun came in through a window over the sink, casting the black engine and the multicolored cars and the red caboose in natural light. It was all completely real.

"Good morning," said Ray as he poured golden eggs into a hot, buttered pan, where the mixture pooled and sizzled pleasantly. The coffee maker sputtered and hissed and filled the kitchen with the black bittersweet smell of coffee. "We need to talk."

Milo blinked and rubbed his eyes. "Alright," he assented. He was prepared for Ray to express concern, to tell him that he, Milo, was unwell, that he was imagining things, that he needed to see a doctor. But Ray apparently had put the events of last night behind him already. There were more pressing matters on his mind.

"You know this is a difficult month for me," he said as he stood gazing into the pan of eggs, holding aloft a rubber spatula. "Well," he went on. "It will all be over soon. Next Wednesday is the night. The anniversary…"

"Ah," said Milo. "Yes, of course."

"I'll want to be alone, but…I'd appreciate it if you could be here. Just knowing you're upstairs. I think it will help me."

"That's no problem," said Milo. "I don't have any plans."

Ray turned and looked at Milo with one of his tight-lipped smiles, his eyes glistening. "Terrific," he said.

Milo nodded, forcing a smile. Apparently Ray was determined to go on acting as if nothing had happened the night before. Milo still did not know what he was going to do, if he was indeed going to move out, find a new place to stay, book an appointment with a psychiatrist, or possibly even a neurologist, or if he would just pretend, like Ray, as if nothing had happened, like the whole situation was perfectly sensible and legitimate.

Ray set mugs of coffee and plates of steaming scrambled eggs on the table. He hummed a merry tune as he squirted ketchup liberally onto his eggs. An image flashed through Milo's brain, a fantasy of stabbing Ray in the throat with a dinner fork, and watching his blood spill out onto the plate like sauce.

The doorbell rang. Uttering a perverse coo of delight, which was muffled by a mouth full of scrambled eggs, Ray pushed himself from the table and went to the front door.

"Isn't it a little early for deliveries?" muttered Milo, at last forcing himself to take a bite of food.

Ray slid the large, rectangular cardboard box into the house, closing the front door behind him. He pushed the package over to the door leading down into the basement, and then returned to his seat at the kitchen table. For weeks Milo had wondered what was inside the mysterious packages which arrived at the house, and which always went directly downstairs, into the basement which Milo had never seen. Now, suddenly, it was obvious.

"Can I open it?" he said.

Ray shrugged, slurping his coffee. "Sure, why not?"

Retrieving a pair of kitchen shears from a drawer, Milo paused for a moment by the table, watching Ray gobble his breakfast. Scissors would be much more effective than a fork, there was no doubt of that.

Ray looked up at him, a bit of egg dangling from his mustache. "Go on, then," he said. "You must be curious what's inside."

Yes, Milo was curious. Not about the package—he'd already guessed what it was—but about Ray. What was inside *him*? What would Milo find if he sliced him open with that pair of shears? Blood and gore? Or the clacking gears and greasy pistons of a hideous machine, wreathed with blue inhuman entrails, plump with some Satanic oil?

Milo sliced open the cardboard package along the seam of translucent tape. There it was, couched in plastic packaging balloons: a bundle of model train tracks, and some other random train parts individually boxed and labeled. Milo put the scissors back in the drawer.

"You should come down into the basement," offered Ray as Milo sat back down to stare at his plate of cooling breakfast. "Don't you want to watch me work?"

"I have my own work to do. I have to start a new commission. But…what do you mean, watch you work? You mean at your job? Or building model trains?"

Ray chuckled. "The trains *are* my job. I told you, I'm an engineer."

"A train engineer…"

"That's right."

Ray smiled, his eyes glowing blue like the headlight of the model train, but still he did not show his teeth.

Next Wednesday? Had Ray misspoken when discussing the anniversary of his dog's demise? So many weeks had already gone by, so many games of gin rummy, so many nights of Ray moaning the beast's filthy name in his sleep. It was Tuesday, or possibly Sunday, so that meant more than another week until it would all be over.

And what about Kyra? When was she getting back? Milo hadn't been sleeping well, or eating well either. He was drinking too much. When had it happened, the revelation about the model train, his confrontation with

Ray? Last night? Or last week? Ray's calendar, hanging in the kitchen, could not be trusted, but nor could Milo's memory. He texted Kyra:

I know this is crazy because we still haven't met. But I feel really close to you. I miss you. Is that crazy? I'm having a rough week. I really can't wait to see you.

It was eight in the morning. Ray had already cleaned up from breakfast and had descended into the basement with his box of model train parts. Milo needed more coffee, he wasn't ready to confront his work yet. Anyway, before focusing on drawing he needed to put together a plan for how exactly he was going to escape from this cursed house, and how he was going to kill Ray.

awww u poor thing :(i'm sorry ur having a bad week. i'm gonna be back soon just hang in there

Disposing of the corpse posed a problem. Ray never left the house, but the delivery agents would notice if he stopped coming to the door to pick up his packages. Sooner or later the police would be called. They'd search the residence and find Ray's body decomposing in the basement amid his model train parts.

Thank you. Honestly, just hearing from you at all is so nice, it gives me the strength to go on with my day haha. I feel better already.

Milo drained the last of the coffee in his mug. Murder fantasies were pleasant, but they solved nothing. What he needed was money. The price tag on the latest commission was substantial. If he could finish it quickly, it would buy him some time to focus on art, to focus on getting sober, getting his life together. That's what he needed.

Milo refilled his mug from the coffee pot and went upstairs.

Sketches for the new commission, which Milo had drawn up the night before, were spread out on his writing desk. Standing over the desk holding his coffee, Milo regarded them with disgust. He seized them, crumpling them in his hand and then shoving them into the waste paper basket. He unscrewed the plastic cap on his bottle of bourbon, poured some into his coffee, drank deeply, and grimaced. Without sugar and cream, whiskey in coffee was far too bitter. Nonetheless, sacrifices had to be made.

The thought of sitting down at his desk and beginning to draw filled Milo with anxiety. He paced back and forth in his room, sipping his foul drink.

The client, who at this point would perhaps more accurately be called a patron considering he was Milo's primary source of income, had been so pleased with Milo's work so far that, for this next piece, he had given his favorite artist carte blanche.

You know me, he'd written in his message to Milo. *You know what I like. All I ask is that you make it big, and bold. I want a masterpiece. Surprise me with your genius.*

Such instructions were, of course, infuriating. It was bad enough to have to devote time to manifesting the unclean hallucinations described in gross detail by this anonymous fetishist, but to be forced to imagine them himself, to exert his genius (for Milo was a genius, secretly he'd always known it, and now he had no choice but to believe it, because he had little else to believe in), to *expend* his genius, toward the invention of some new, ghastly scenario, which was meant to exceed the others in the audacity of its morbid perversion—it was degrading. And yet the bounty on this "masterpiece" was such that Milo could hardly refuse.

He finished his coffee, went downstairs to refill his mug. The model train that sometimes raced around the perimeters of the house was creeping slowly. Milo felt like it was following him, watching him, as he drained the coffee pot into his mug and then rinsed it out in the sink. In his room, he stuffed the dark portals with winter coats and sweaters to prevent the train from entering. Then, pouring some bourbon into his coffee, he laid out on his desk the fresh pad of large easel paper which he'd purchased for this assignment. Rather than wasting time with more sketches, he was just going to begin drawing. The bourbon had begun to have its desired effect, the holy spirit of devil-may-care which was the prerequisite for all creation.

The client liked trains, so Milo would draw trains. He set his pencil to the paper and began to sketch the tracks.

Late in the afternoon Milo left the house to get more bourbon. Tramping down the sidewalk toward the liquor store, he smoked a cigarette. Nicotine sharpened the dreams of alcohol and relaxed the jaw of caffeine. The piece was taking shape, though as he drank his lines grew freer and more ironic, no longer simply grotesque thematically, but formally. The pylons in the background loomed and leered like the demonic skeletons of eagles, their industrial brains linked together by medical electrodes.

"Pick that up."

Stunned, blinking, Milo looked up to meet the eyes of a middle-aged man, plump and ruddy, who was out walking his boxer terrier.

"What?"

"Your cigarette butt."

The man pointed to the butt, still glowing orange, which Milo had just tossed into the street—an action which, in the city, hardly would have been noticed by anyone.

Milo gazed into the man's eyes, slowly realizing that he was, in fact, entirely serious.

"Are you deaf?" repeated the villain. "There's a $500 fine for littering."

"Your dog is ugly," said Milo with savage idiocy, the words crumbling from his lips like unswallowed food. "Your whole family is ugly."

The man's pink face glowed red. Milo walked past him, lighting another cigarette.

Milo worked furiously. Ray left a plate of lasagna outside his bedroom door, but the caffeine and nicotine had killed Milo's appetite, and besides, he was too caught up with drawing. Would the client feel betrayed, ripped off, insulted? Was Milo, who with each stroke of the pencil seemed to add fresh depths of lunacy to this drawing, making a mockery of this man's darkest secrets? He didn't care. All that mattered was that he finished it, whatever *it* was.

Milo worked furiously, drank and smoked furiously, late into the night.

Milo jumped. He'd been dreaming.

Groaning, he pushed himself up from his desk. Where his cheek had been resting on the drawing paper there was a stream of drool which had blotted and smeared his lines. Milo's head was pounding. He pushed the architect lamp toward the wall to spare his eyes, and stumbled out of his chair. He needed water. That's when he heard it.

"Maxine…*Maxine!*"

Ray's night terrors had returned, but Milo thought he detected a note of urgency, of real waking fear, in Ray's moans. He didn't like the idea of getting any closer to that racket, but he was desperately thirsty.

"Maxine…Come on, Maxine. Let's see the train!"

The freight train whistle bellowed outside, and the little model freight train whistled in response from some corner of the house. Ray must have flipped a track switch, so that the model train could make its circuit of the house while skipping Milo's room now that he'd blocked off the tunnels. Milo hesitated at the top of the stairs. He could drink from the bathroom tap, but it tasted like chlorine and nickel. The kitchen faucet had a filter attachment.

"Come on Maxine, let's try to catch it! Haha!"

Something must have clicked in Ray's dream, because suddenly he didn't sound frightened but positively ecstatic. He must have been reliving some pleasant memory. Milo descended the stairs.

"Haha, isn't this terrific! Look, there, it's coming, the train is coming, Maxine!"

At the base of the stairs Milo froze. There he was, Ray, in his underwear, without his glasses, his hair disheveled. He was beneath the oil painting of Maxine, gazing up at it with a frantic smile, his jaw hanging open.

"Come on Maxine, here it comes. Are you ready?"

Outside, in the night, the freight train bellowed again, and the model train replied in turn. And then it emerged in the living room, whistling and clacking on its metal track along the wall.

Ray began to chase after the model train in the semblance of a jog, waving his hand and calling to the ghost of Maxine. But then, as the train turned around the corner, Ray began to shout with terror:

"Maxine, no! Don't go onto the track! Maxine! No! *MAXINE!!!*"

Train whistles merged with Ray's mortal scream as he fell to his knees, stretching out his arms. He screamed until his face was red and swollen, but just when Milo thought that he would break down into a fit of sobbing, instead he wobbled to his feet, and, with a howl of rage, clambered onto the antique credenza where at that moment the model train was passing by and, seizing the miniature locomotive in his hands, like some freakish hairless Kong he ripped it from the tracks, pulling the train of cars behind it, and hurled it to the ground. Grabbing one of the train cars left behind, he used it like a cudgel to begin smashing up the tracks, howling all the while like a beast. Bits of plastic and metal, and droplets from Ray's foaming mouth, were flying everywhere.

Milo had seen enough. He went into the kitchen and, first taking up the pair of kitchen shears from the drawer for good measure, filled a cup of cold water, gulped it down hastily while listening to make sure Ray was still in the other room, and then refilled it and downed it again.

It was impossible at this point for Milo to be shocked or frightened by anything. As a child he had suspected that the world was a bleak and hellish place, a dark wilderness of meaningless pleasure and suffering dotted with the gleaming castles of the rich, where they and their sycophants entertained the fantasy of civilization at the expense of everyone else. As he grew older he allowed himself to be convinced otherwise, to see life, perhaps, the way that other people saw it, as a pleasant thing worth living—the only evidence for this being the fleeting illusions of a woman's affections. But once these were withdrawn, like the snuffing of a lantern, the world was black again, and it was back to the cold facts of sheer existence.

Gripping the sheers by the blade, Milo tapped the handle thoughtfully against the kitchen counter while he listened to the tumult of rage in the other room. That's when he noticed the door to the cellar, for the first time, was standing wide open. A grisly realization flashed through Milo's brain, and it suddenly occurred to him that he must investigate the basement straightaway, now while Ray remained in his fit of distraction.

The wooden stairs were exceedingly steep and narrow, and creaked with every step. They descended to a large basement which had been carpeted in forest green. The walls, covered in faux-wood paneling, were adorned with framed art. Along one wall was a workbench and shelves filled with tools and model train parts. In the center of the room was a model train set, the old-fashioned kind on a large table.

The miniature town, through which the train tracks ran, was instantly recognizable: it was the very stretch of suburbs where they lived. At the center of it was the train station; across the tracks from there, Ray's house, and all the other houses on the street, reproduced with striking verisimilitude. There, standing in the lawn in front of Ray's house, was Ray himself, a wooden figurine dressed in little fabric garments. The same mustache, the same glasses, the same neatly ironed shirt tucked into chinos. And, next to him, a black schnauzer, Maxine.

Milo thought he noticed something through the window in the second floor of the model house. So, grabbing the roof, he found it lifted off easily. There, in the spare bedroom, bent over a desk, was little Milo, wearing gym shorts and an old t-shirt, hard at work over a drawing of a train, with a half-empty bottle of whiskey beside him. Tiny model train tracks were laced around the perimeter of his bedroom wall, and throughout the whole house.

Smiling, Milo leaned the roof up against the side of the house. This was not what he'd come looking for. It was the art on the walls which he wanted to see. His art. Milo's art. They were not the originals, of course—Milo scanned all of the pieces at the print shop and uploaded them to the commission website, but each one of them had then been printed out and framed.

Yes, there they were, every last piece. Milo walked from frame to frame, inspecting them: the loathsome drawings he'd been producing for, how long now? Weeks, months, years? Little locomotives with cycloptic human eyes crawling over the naked body of a sleeping woman.

Men and women penetrating and being penetrated by engines. Tongues that were tracks, eyes that billowed smoke, breasts that were railroad crossing lights. A Satanic communion of sex and machines. Why had it taken him so long to guess that Ray had been behind it, that Ray had been behind everything?

It suddenly occurred to Milo that things had gone quiet upstairs. The hair on the back of his neck stood up and he slowly turned around.

Ray was standing at the bottom of the basement stairs. He'd found his glasses, but he was still naked except for his underwear. He was covered in sweat from his rampage, and his hands were bloody from attacking the metal trains.

"You're the only one who understands me," said Ray, his mustache drooping with sad exhaustion. "You've been through a lot, and so have I. You lost someone special to you, just like me. You're a terrific artist. I've commissioned work from so many people, but no one's ever got it right, until you. You've made my dreams become real."

"I'm going to sleep, Ray," said Milo, fingering the scissors. "Excuse me."

Ray didn't budge from where he stood, blocking the stairs.

"Don't be like that, Milo…You're not mad at me, are you? Did I do something wrong? This is a difficult month for me…"

Milo raised the scissors, holding them up for Ray to see.

"It would be tragic," said Milo, enunciating each word slowly, "if something were to happen to that beautiful portrait of Maxine."

Ray gasped and cowered, covering his mouth with one hand and throwing himself back up against the wall. His hands trembled.

"You would never…" his voice muffled by his hand, "you're an artist…"

"No one is more prepared to destroy art than an artist. We are gods. We create and we destroy. I am a god, do you understand me, Ray?"

Ray sank to the floor, still covering his mouth. He nodded impotently.

"Now listen to me," said Milo, taking a step forward. He was still holding up the scissors, which in that moment had become the talisman of his apotheosis, like the crook and flail of Osiris, the rod of Mercury. "I am going to complete the final drawing, as per our arrangement," he went on. "And it will be a *masterpiece*, as per our arrangement. Such a masterpiece, in fact, that you are going to pay me *triple* your original offer."

"But…"

"Silence," hissed Milo. He brandished the scissors at Ray like a crucifix at a vampire. "Whatever dragon hoard of gold you've stashed away is enough so that you don't have to work like the rest of us. You've got money somewhere, money you inherited along with this house. And it is *owed* to me. It is a tiny *fraction* of what is owed to me. So we're going to forget about what happened tonight. Tomorrow morning we'll be friends. Everything will be normal. But you and your trains are not to enter my room. You are not even to look at the *model* of my room. Have I been understood?"

Ray nodded, his eyes squeezed tight like a child trying to wish away the horrors of the world.

"Goodnight, Ray."

For good measure, Milo barricaded his bedroom door with the dresser, and left the scissors on his nightstand. He fell asleep a minute before daybreak.

hey r u okay?

Milo…

text me at some point so i know ur okay :/

Milo had only managed a couple of hours of sleep before he was awakened by the sound and smell of bacon sizzling downstairs, and Ray whistling cheerfully. Looking at his phone, he saw these cryptic messages from Kyra and immediately texted her back.

Hey, I'm fine. Sorry I didn't see this sooner. What's going on?

Milo dragged himself out of bed, pushed the dresser aside to free himself from the bedroom, and took a shower. His entire body ached, like he'd been beaten all over with a sack of apples. It was a cold morning, and when he got dressed he pulled on a sweater—the first sweater of the season. While he was in the shower, Kyra had replied:

u posted some stuff that made me worried
just wanted to check in on u

"Good morning, Milo!" Ray smiled his usual smile and went right back to whistling. The train wreckage in the living room had all been cleared away, but somehow Ray looked perfectly well-rested. Milo poured himself a cup of coffee and sat down at the kitchen table, pulling up his social media profile to try and figure out what Kyra was talking about.

There it was…a shadowy picture of his hand, gripping the pair of scissors. He must have taken it at some point last night. Milo broke out in a cold sweat when he read the caption, which he had no memory of having written:

I am the God of Death. I will cut open my own life. I will dismember myself and recreate the universe from the bloody pieces of my dead body.

"Wake up and smell the bacon!" Ray set the plate of bacon, scrambled eggs, and golden buttered toast in front of Milo. "You know the rules, no phones at the table."

Milo was not only embarrassed, but frightened by the gap in his memory. He discovered, moreover, that he'd done substantial work on the drawing at some point in the night. But when? How was that possible? Had it only been one night, or had a whole day or week transpired since the revelations in the basement?

In any case, Milo felt like he hadn't slept in days. He was almost finished with his second cup of coffee but he felt on the verge of falling asleep. But he had to work. He had to finish it…

The piece was coming along, at least. The raptorial pylons lorded over a neurasthenic wasteland like predators or voyeurs, and beneath them…what was it? A trainwreck? An orgy? A graveyard? Milo's bedroom? Milo's dream…

It was obvious he was drinking too much, but nonetheless his years of study, and the countless hours of intense practice that summer, shone through the haze of alcohol. As much as Milo hated to admit it, the work was good. It was like his talents, having lain in some dormancy of transmutation, now thrummed and strained their wings against an invisible cocoon which now cracked and oozed ink-like blood. Some loathsome moth-like thing was struggling to be born.

Days went by in a blur of nicotine, coffee, and bourbon. Milo finished the lines, and then attacked the colors with drunk, delirious irony. Kyra was back from California or South Carolina or wherever she'd been, and Milo was going to meet her in a couple of days. In a couple of days, he would be done with the piece, he'd get paid, he'd meet Kyra, they'd fall in love, he'd find another place to live, he'd begin, he'd begin a new life, finally, in a couple of days he'd be free.

"I'm going into the city today," said Milo as Ray set the plate of French toast, topped with sliced strawberries and dusted with powdered sugar and draped with ribbons of maple syrup, down on the table in front of him.

"I thought we'd play cards tonight," replied Ray doubtfully. The model train announced its arrival in the kitchen with a playful toot of the whistle.

Milo bared his teeth unpleasantly. "I can't really say for sure, Ray. I don't know where the night will take me."

"I see. You must be meeting your girlfriend."

"Yes, that's right." Milo was feeling sadistic. He'd finished the drawing, uploaded it to the website late last night. Soon he'd be flush with cash, enough to get out of this place, enough to start over, again.

"I finished the drawing," said Milo as he chewed his meal. Ray bristled. It was the first time the subject had been broached since the night in the basement.

"I'll take a look, right after breakfast."

"And you'll pay me right away, yes?"

"Sure thing, Milo." Ray, tired and faintly sad, smiled pityingly as if Milo were an aging and senile parent slowly expiring in hospice care.

By the time Milo had trimmed his beard, showered, got dressed in his nicest shirt, brushed his hair, and rubbed cologne on his wrists and neck, he'd had the equivalent of two, possibly three bourbons. The last week, the last month had been a blur, but this was it. He was meeting Kyra, at long last. He had saved enough money to at last free himself from the grasp of the loathsome incubus in whose nightmare he was imprisoned, and now he would begin in earnest on his own work, his *real* work.

He fell asleep on the train, gazing out at pylons, cables, smokestacks.

i'm so sorry to do this to u but i cant do this. ur a really sweet person but i jus dont feel comfy with this. i wish you all the best

"Last stop, last stop!"

Milo was frozen, barely awake from his nap, staring at Kyra's message. He re-read it three, four, five times.

"Sir, this is the last stop, I have to ask you to please get off the train."

Kyra's message wasn't the only one. Derrick and a couple other old friends, even Acacia, had sent him messages over the course of the morning, and Milo quickly figured out why.

The drawing. His *masterpiece*…He hadn't just uploaded it to the commission website. Somehow, in a state of drunken, overworked, sleep-deprived delirium, he'd posted it on his social media profile for everyone to see. And everyone had seen it…

Milo looked at the piece as if for the first time. He could barely remember drawing most of it. It was like the hells of Hieronymous Bosch, a nightmare rife with desolate ecstasies, shameless transfigurations stained with blood and sex. But it was worse, much worse than the fantasies of Bosch, because it was not meant to be art, but pornography, and it was recognizable as such, forcing one to reflect on what tortured, fallen soul could possibly regard such horrors with delectation.

Because the train station functioned as a de facto shelter for the insane and indigent, all those lost and tainted souls expelled from respectable society, there were no chairs or benches in the whole sprawling complex. There couldn't be, because otherwise they'd be used as beds by the homeless. And so the poor, elderly, crippled, and mentally cracked detritus of the city who sought refuge in the labyrinthine caverns of the station were forced to sleep on the floor like feral dogs. That's where Milo found himself, because he had nowhere else to be. Sitting on the floor, staring at the messages on his phone:

Hey man how you been? You doing okay?

Milo we need to talk, call me please.

Worried about you, buddy. Been trying to get in touch. Can you let me know you're okay?

Milo began to laugh, and it occurred to him that passersby might see him sitting there on the floor and laughing like a lunatic and conclude that he, Milo, was another half-crazed castaway, one of the scorned ones, the invisible ones, the untouchables, the exiles. And this made him laugh even harder.

There was no sense in wasting a trip to the city. It was nice to get out of the suburbs and stretch one's legs. Besides, it was payday, and there were things one could buy here that weren't easily available elsewhere: electric bonesaws, for example, and hydrochloric acid.

The first order of business, of course, was drinking. Milo's favorite bar didn't open until the afternoon, so he went to a family chain restaurant advertising a special on margaritas.

"Deep down I think I've always been a tequila man." He smiled recklessly at the waitress. "I'd like a margarita, please. It's two for the price of one, right? Can you bring them out at the same time?"

Maybe bourbon really had been the problem all along. Tequila was clear, and Milo needed to clear his mind. Crimes of vast religious magnitude presented themselves to his imagination as he sipped the first cocktail. The kind of violent projects he'd entertained for days or weeks but had managed to repress now appeared with lucid grandeur in his mind's eye: dazzling, resplendent dreamscapes of serene cruelty, entire cities and universes of pain.

Dear Kyra. Thank you for letting me know. It was wonderful getting to know you. I won't bother you anymore.

Milo was trembling as he composed this message. He felt like he would vomit, but he didn't. He had thought Kyra was different, he had thought she would recognize his heart, his tortured, pagan spirit, his wild kingdom. But now she had glimpsed it, she had glimpsed his wild kingdom and judged it to be unclean. He finished the first margarita and, wiping the moisture from the corner of his eyes, started eagerly on the second. What was to be done?

He had never thought of himself as a murderer, mere months ago he never would have dreamed that he would be capable of it, but the idea of killing and dismembering Ray, and possibly setting fire to or blowing up his house, now impressed itself on Milo's mind so urgently that he was forced not just to indulge it as a pleasant fantasy but to really consider it as a course of action. Were there not better targets, politically speaking, for Milo's suicidal revenge? Certainly, but there was nothing, absolutely nothing that would feel quite as satisfying as destroying Ray, his trains, and those disgusting drawings.

Milo did not want to hurt Acacia, Kyra, Derrick, or anyone else who had abandoned him. He just wanted them to suffer, from a distance, the brutal majesty of his annihilation.

Wasn't there so much to live for? What about being an artist? No, not after posting that image online. His reputation was ruined. There was no way to play it off as some kind of prank. It was close enough to Milo's usual style that anyone would be able to recognize it as his work, his lines, his colors.

Human existence was divided between pagan forests and madhouses. The schools, corporations, prisons, and art galleries all were varieties of madhouses, dedicated to violently controlling man's innate cruelty and insanity. Milo had tried to leave the madhouse, to go and live in the forest, to be a free person, and he had failed. His failure had not even been dramatic, just slow and idiotic. Some people are meant for the madhouse, to work and suffer, to watch television, to be quiet, to be cuckolded. Milo had made the mistake of thinking he was cut out for art. But he should have stayed in the city, should have stayed at the scented candle shop, should have never argued with Acacia but should have let her do whatever she wanted. Now everything had fallen to pieces. His life was a sordid mess, an abortion. He was getting old, getting fat, he was an alcoholic, he was half-insane, he was a loser, a failure, a trainwreck.

Milo still had the wherewithal to order another two margaritas without appearing wasted or deranged. He needed the tequila. He needed the courage. He wasn't going out to buy a sword to bring home and use to kill his landlord. His biography was pathetic enough already, why end it all with an act of utter cowardice? No, he was going to die with dignity. After these drinks, he was going to walk down to the subway station and throw himself in front of a train.

The summer was over. How could one tell? The women in the street, instead of iced coffees in clear plastic, now some of them were clutching white paper cups of hot coffee. It must have been about fifty degrees Fahrenheit, Milo's favorite kind of weather. He and Acacia used to go for walks on days just like this when they first moved to the city together, when the city was still like a dream or a film to them, still Paris in the afternoon, Berlin at night, Tokyo in the morning, before it all became routine, before it all became old.

What would he put in his suicide note? Something elegant and dignified. *I regret nothing.* Or, why not the classic *Goodbye, cruel world?* It expressed everything beautifully. It wasn't a cliché, it was a line of poetry that belonged to everyone.

The subway station was mostly empty. Milo stood on the edge of the platform, which was painted yellow to caution people from standing too close. The track below was littered with plastic soda cups, greasy hamburger bags, a woman's shoe.

According to the electronic sign, the next train was three minutes away.

Was Milo really going to do it? Suicide was absurd, and unnecessary—but then again, so was all of life. An obese, bluish rat with a bright red wound on its haunch scampered out from beneath a white paper bag, crossed the tracks, and disappeared through a hole in the black cement. The rat was able to live in misery because it had no reason to live. Existence was its own justification. Not so for men.

Rays of slanted light shot down through grates above the rails. Milo decided he would focus on these rays of light whenever he jumped. He wasn't angry with anyone anymore. He didn't want revenge. He just didn't want to live anymore. Maybe that was it, his note…maybe that would say everything that needed to be said, without irony or bitterness, so that his memory would not haunt the world but could rest in peace.

This is not my revenge. I just don't want to live anymore. I'm sorry. Goodbye.

The train was one minute away. Milo opened his phone to type out and post his last words. Among the new messages of distress, condemnation, and mockery, from friends, acquaintances, and random strangers, messages which Milo did not bother to look at, he noticed something in his inbox from the official account of Garrote Wire Gallery.

Hey Milo! This is Anastasia with Garrote Wire. A friend sent me the piece you posted last night and we've all been talking about it at the gallery this morning. We're absolutely floored! We'd like to invite you to be part of a group show we're putting together this fall featuring young transgressive artists. Would you be interested in showing this piece? Let me know!

Oh, and one other thing. The show is reserved for artists under 30—does that include you?

Numbly, gingerly, Milo typed out his reply:

Yeah. I'm 29.

The train rushed past inches from Milo's face, blowing the hot tears from his cheeks with a roar of cold, subterranean wind.

Ray was not himself at dinner. Dark thoughts clouded his face.

"I sent you the money," he said at one point as he picked at his tuna casserole. "I don't expect I'll be wanting…anything more."

"What's wrong?" said Milo, who had picked up a six-pack of expensive Belgian ale on his way home, and which he was now guzzling to wash down his second helping of casserole. "You didn't like it?"

After dinner, Milo noticed that the model train tracks which previously had ran along the walls of the house, and the tunnels leading in and out of each room, all of it had vanished without a trace. It was like they had never been there at all.

That night he slept as soundly as a grizzly bear. When the freight train blasted its monastic horn, Milo did not awaken, but smiled in his sleep.

The next morning, Milo opened another message from Anastasia from Garrote Wire:

Perfect! We look forward to working with you. By the way, what's the title of the piece?

Milo was lying in bed. He stared at the ceiling for several minutes and then, a smile creeping into his lips, replied:

I call it, "Milo's Commute."

Ray wasn't in the mood to make breakfast. Uncharacteristically unshaven, a shadow of stubble across his cheeks, he stared into his bowl of breakfast cereal and watched it slowly grow soggy.

"Do you think," he muttered, "you'll stay on through the winter?"

"Nothing is permanent in this world, Ray. *Nothing.*" Shamelessly, Milo had brought his nearly-empty bottle of bourbon down to the breakfast table, and presently poured all that remained of it into his cup of black coffee as he began to chuckle to himself like an idiot. "This is just the beginning of my journey. Just one *station*. The first of my *Stations of the Cross!*"

Acknowledgements

I would like to thank Nick Vyssotsky, Ryan Maleady, Garrett Phelps, Nate Sloan, and Ryan Borzoie for their kindness and support when I had just moved to New York and was finishing this manuscript; Greg Howard, whose fiction workshop was the birthplace of "The Brooms of Carlack"; J.W. McCormack at *The Baffler* where an earlier version of "The Necromancer's Driver" was first published; Manuel Marrero and Scott Litts at *Expat Press*; *DoNotResearch* and the DNR community; Anna Sebastian for the use of her brilliant painting as the cover of this book; Udith Dematagoda, Richard Porteous, Stewart McCarthy, and Lydia Sviatoslavsky at Hyperidean; my students past and future; Andrew Patton and Matthias Roth for their enduring support (and Matthias for giving me license to turn his nightmares into fiction); my parents, my brothers Zac and Gabe, and my sisters Bereket and Rachel; and for her patience, while it lasted, Maia, and our cats Trismegistus and Orpheus.